Presents

Take a look at our books for September!

A marriage ended or a marriage mended? Kayla
has been bought back by her estranged husband,
billionaire Duardo Alvarez, in Helen Bianchin's
scorcher *Purchased by the Billionaire*. Bedded
for revenge or wedded for passion? Freya has
made the mistake of hiding the existence of Italian
Enrico Ranieri's little son, and she must make amends
as his convenient wife in Michelle Reid's torrid tale
The Ranieri Bride. Is revenge sweet? Greek tycoon
Christos Carides certainly thinks so when he seduces
Becca Summer in Kim Lawrence's sizzling story,
The Carides Pregnancy. But for how long? Out for
the count? Italian aristocrat Alessio Ramontella
certainly thinks he's KO'd innocent English beauty
Laura, but will she actually succumb to his ruthless
seduction? Find out in *The Count's Blackmail Bargain*
by Sara Craven. Meantime, Carol Marinelli's mixing
business with intense pleasure in her new UNCUT
novel, *Taken for His Pleasure*. It's a gold band of
blackmail for temporary bride Maddison as she's
forced to marry wealthy Greek Demetrius Papasakis
in *The Greek's Convenient Wife* by Melanie Milburne.
Mistress material? Nora Lang doesn't think she's got
what it takes in Susan Napier's *Mistress for a Weekend*.
But tycoon Blake MacLeod thinks Nora definitely has
something special—confidential information. And
he'll keep her in his bed to prevent her giving it away.
Finally, an ultimatum…*The Marriage Ultimatum* by
Helen Brooks. It's Carter Blake's only option when
Liberty refuses to let him take her.

EXPECTING!

She's sexy,
successful...
and
PREGNANT!

Relax and enjoy our fabulous series about
couples whose passion ends in pregnancies...
sometimes unexpected! Of course, the birth
of a baby is always a joyful event, and we can
guarantee that our characters will become
wonderful moms and dads—but what
happened in those nine months before?

Share the surprises, emotions, drama and
suspense as our parents-to-be come to terms
with the prospect of bringing a new baby
into the world. All will discover that the
business of making babies brings with it
the most special love of all....

Delivered only by Harlequin Presents®

Kim Lawrence

THE CARIDES PREGNANCY

EXPECTING!

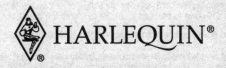

HARLEQUIN®

TORONTO • NEW YORK • LONDON
AMSTERDAM • PARIS • SYDNEY • HAMBURG
STOCKHOLM • ATHENS • TOKYO • MILAN • MADRID
PRAGUE • WARSAW • BUDAPEST • AUCKLAND

ISBN-13: 978-0-373-12565-4
ISBN-10:   0-373-12565-8

THE CARIDES PREGNANCY

First North American Publication 2006.

Copyright © 2005 by Kim Lawrence.

www.eHarlequin.com

Printed in U.S.A.

All about the author...
Kim Lawrence

Though lacking much authentic Welsh blood, **KIM LAWRENCE** comes from English/Irish stock. She was born and brought up in north Wales. She returned there when she married, and her sons were both born on Anglesey, an island off the coast. Though not isolated, Anglesey is a little off the beaten track, but lively Dublin, which Kim loves, is only a short ferry ride away.

Today they live on the farm her husband was brought up on. Welsh is the first language of many people in this area, and Kim's husband and sons are all bilingual—she is having a lot of fun, not to mention a few headaches, trying to learn the language!

With small children, the unsocial hours of nursing didn't look attractive, so encouraged by a husband who thinks she can do anything she sets her mind to, Kim tried her hand at writing. Always a keen Harlequin reader, it seemed natural for her to write a romance novel—now she can't imagine doing anything else.

She is a keen gardener and cook, and enjoys running—often on the beach, as living on an island the sea is never very far away. She is usually accompanied by her Jack Russell, Sprout—don't ask, it's a long story!

CHAPTER ONE

CARL STONE'S control over his financial empire was total, whereas the weather in the Home Counties, for the moment, remained outside his dominion.

It was the day of his only daughter's wedding, and the Met Office had predicted an early snowfall across the country. The ominous clouds overhead suggested that promise would almost definitely be fulfilled.

Sure enough, as a sprinkling of early guests began to arrive, making their way through the tight security cordon around the Cathedral, the first thick white flakes began to fall.

A few snowflakes, however, were not about to dampen the spirits of these guests. Most would have happily struggled through a total white-out, weighed down by their understated—in some cases overstated—elegance, their designer hats, fur coats, and jewels, to attend what was extravagantly being billed as the society wedding of the year!

Only one person appeared not to appreciate his good fortune at being there. The tall, lean figure stood a little apart, with one hand thrust negligently into his trouser pocket, his broad back set against the gnarled trunk of an ancient yew. He was apparently oblivious to the biting cold wind, and the snow that had begun to dust his dark hair and the shoulders of his well-cut morning suit.

If the expression on his dark, startlingly handsome face suggested anything it was intense boredom. This sombreness of expression was lightened occasionally when he responded in kind to a greeting from a friend or family member as they passed by.

One impressionable young lady, gasping as she witnessed such a moment, was heard to declare fervently that she would happily sell her soul to be on the receiving end of that smile. Her more literally-minded sister retorted bluntly that she would like to be on the receiving end of more than his smile!

'Jocasta… India… Behave, girls.' Herding her sulky daughters ahead of her, their mother—a long way from indifferent herself to the attributes of the tall, enigmatic figure with the fallen angel features and the dangerous sexy aura—gave a slightly wistful glance in his direction before following her offspring inside the splendid Gothic edifice.

If others present had been unaware of his identity, his colouring would have immediately placed him on the groom's guest list. *Typically Greek*, they would have said, observing his jet-black hair, warm olive skin, and a profile that could have come straight from an ancient Greek statue. But those better acquainted could have told them that this man wasn't *typically* anything!

The question of identity didn't arise, however, because of course there was hardly a soul amongst the socially prominent guests who wasn't aware of his identity. Any number, if asked, could probably list his star sign, his shoe size, and hazard an educated guess at his bank balance.

Christos Carides, head of the Carides Empire, was actually as instantly recognisable to his fellow guests as was their host, and according to some sources he was even more disgustingly rich! And, it went without saying, *much* better looking.

Despite outward appearances Christos *was* feeling the cold, having spent the last month enjoying warm Australian sunshine, he was keenly aware of the chill in the air. A chill that was very nearly as bone-biting as the one between him and his cousin—the groom.

A spasm of contempt briefly distorted the perfect contours of his sensually moulded lips as his thoughts touched on the subject of his cousin Alex.

At that moment a shortish, cherubic-faced and fair-haired young man emerged from the side of the building. He gave a relieved sigh as he immediately spotted the person he was looking for. Breathless, his jacket flapping open to reveal a striped silk waistcoat, the harassed best man belted along the path, narrowly avoiding several collisions with startled-looking guests.

'I'm Peter,' he blurted out as he skidded to halt in front of the tall, commanding figure of the Greek financier.

'Yes, I remember. You're Carl's godson, aren't you...?'

Peter nodded. 'I'm the best man after...' He stopped, looking uncomfortable.

Christos helped him out. 'After I refused.'

'Yeah, well, you don't know how glad I am to see you.'

'Always glad to make someone happy,' Christos observed drily. 'Can I help you?' he prompted, when the younger man didn't respond.

'You've got to come with me!'

In response to this dramatic statement Christos flexed his shoulders and levered himself with effortless elegance from the tree trunk. 'I have...?' he murmured politely.

The sardonic inflection and the cold light in the dark, deepset eyes that rested on his face caused the breathless younger man's hopeful smile to gutter and fade. This was not a promising start.

'He's asking for you. Please...Mr C-Carides,' he stuttered. 'I don't know what to do. He's a total mess, and if Uncle Carl sees him like this there'll be hell to pay,' he predicted gloomily. 'He drank enough to sink a battleship last night. He really isn't himself.'

Christos did not display surprise—because he *wasn't* surprised. He would have been more surprised if his cousin *hadn't* fallen off the wagon. At times of stress—and presumably marrying the heiress of one of the richest men in Britain came under that title—his cousin always reached for a crutch.

'I think you'll find, Peter, when you have known Alex a little longer, that he *is* being himself.'

He would learn, as people generally did, that underneath the charm Alex possessed in abundance his cousin was essentially weak and, like many insecure men, inclined to be spiteful and manipulative when thwarted.

The younger man looked a little nonplussed by the languid response. 'I don't think you understand. He can hardly stand up and he keeps...' He paused and glanced over his shoulder. *'Crying...'*

It was clear to Christos that in the young Englishman's eyes these masculine tears were the most embarrassing feature of this situation. 'And this should concern me because...?' he enquired, in his deep, accented drawl.

The younger man's expression betrayed his shock and revulsion at this casual response. 'You're not going to help?'

The reply, when it came, was unambiguous. 'No.'

Under normal circumstances the younger man would not have dared speak his mind to the likes of Christos Carid but the realisation that he was going to have to sort out mess himself made him recklessly outspoken.

'When Alex said you were a cold, callous bastard I ga you the benefit of the doubt!'

Christos smiled, revealing even white teeth and z warmth. 'Your mistake, I think,' he observed mildly. you want my advice, for what it's worth, I'd shove his he in a bucket of ice water, fill another with black coffee a force-feed it to him.

'Don't worry too much,' he added. 'He has the consti-
tution of a hospital superbug. Now, if you'll excuse me,
I'm waiting for someone.' With a slight inclination of his
dark head he dismissed the younger man.

The stressed best man retreated a few feet, then turned
back, his resentment roughening his young voice as he
yelled back, 'Uncle Carl is right. You and the rest of
Carides family may think you're a cut above everyone else,
but when it comes down to it you're no better than a
damned pirate. No morals, no scruples and no manners.'

Peter saw that, rather than being offended by the insult-
ing tirade, Christos was grinning, in that instant looking
every inch a swashbuckling buccaneer—one, furthermore,
likely to cut his throat on a whim!

'Is that a direct quote?'

Peter was not a physical young man, but the mockery
gleaming in the Greek's dark eyes filled with him with an
uncharacteristic desire to resort to physical violence. Not
that he did, of course. He was angry, not insane! This was
no sedentary businessman he was talking to. Christos
Carides was only in his early thirties, and besides, he had
to be six five if he was an inch—and he definitely worked
out!

Cooling down slightly, Peter became belatedly aware
that people were staring. And, being much less comfortable
with this attention than his adversary, the young man gritted
his teeth and stalked off with as much dignity as he could
muster.

He would have been comforted to know that there was
someone close by who would have applauded his reading
of the Carides character—and added a few choice obser-
vations of her own!

Becca Summer, mingling with guests, was approaching the
security cordon. At that moment her throat was so dry with

nerves she probably couldn't have strung two words together, and if she had she wouldn't have been able to hear what she said above the heavy thud of her pounding heart. Six weeks earlier she hadn't been similarly hindered.

Six weeks earlier she had been uncharacteristically vocal!

'People like these Carides,' she had declared, snarling the name contemptuously. 'They make me sick! They think that just because they have money and power they can do anything they want.' She'd looked at her sister, Erica, and swallowed past the emotional lump in her throat. 'Regardless of who they hurt.'

'You know, Becca, there's not much point being mad,' Erica had pointed out defeatedly.

'You mean don't get mad, get even?' The old cliché had never made more sense to her than it had at that moment.

'Get even?' Erica had exclaimed with a laugh. 'Are you serious? We're talking about the Carides.'

'So you think that people like the Carides imagine they can do anything they want?' Becca had retorted.

'I *know* they can, Becca.'

The bleak retort had made Becca's eyes fill. She'd struggled to hold back the tears and declared fiercely, 'One day I'll teach them that they can't walk all over people and get away with it! You see if I don't.'

It had been said in the heat of the moment, and deep down she probably hadn't really believed that such an opportunity would arise—but here she was, about to do her small part in balancing the scales of justice.

And she was already regretting it big-time!

Becca caught a passer-by staring at her head and quickly pulled off the knitted cloche—not the sort of head gear that people wore to posh weddings—crammed over her tangled titian hair. Pulling a not quite steady hand through her Pre-

Raphaelite curls, she shook her hair back, letting it fan over the dark material of her coat.

Don't give up the day job, Becca. Undercover work is definitely not for you, she told herself, repressing a worried grin.

Part of the problem was that she was not just scared out of her mind, she was exhausted. Hardly surprising, considering that the previous evening she had jumped in her ancient Beetle and driven through the night, halfway across the country, to get here.

Adrenaline and outrage—and seeing the newspaper article concerning the 'society wedding of the year' had given her a double dose of both—could, she discovered, take a protective big sister a long way.

Cars, on the other hand, needed petrol—which was why she had had to walk five miles along a lonely road to the nearest service station at three in the morning. A terrifying experience. And then, just to add to her misery, it had started to snow.

Snow in early November—how unlucky was that?

She had a blister on her right heel to bear witness to her trek, and a suspicion that spontaneity wasn't all it was cracked up to be. After this was over it would be a relief to go back to her normal sensible, cautious, consequence-considering self!

Reckless just wasn't *her*. It wasn't in her nature to throw caution to the wind. In fact, her inability to be spontaneous had been one of the reasons Roger had cited for the failure of their relationship.

Her family and friends had been suitably supportive when the announcement—the very week following their break-up—of Roger's engagement to a bubbly blonde had appeared in the local paper. Becca, uneasily aware that as the dumped fiancée she ought to be feeling more traumatised, had received their sympathy with a degree of guilt.

After a few weeks the role of pathetic victim had begun to get wearing.

When she had said as much to her sister, Erica had said, 'Don't worry—in a few weeks' time they will have a new juicy scandal to talk about.'

Neither of them had suspected at the time that it would be Erica who supplied the scandal!

Erica had told her family about her unplanned pregnancy the same day the ambulance had been called, its sirens ringing, to the neat Edwardian semi where Becca and Erica had grown up

But it had been too late to save the baby.

Later, back home, with the promise that—all being well—their youngest daughter could be discharged the next day, the Summers family had sat down in the sitting room, staring mutely at one another.

Recognising her elderly parents were still in shock—her father was ten years older than her mother, and Elspeth Summer had been forty-five when her younger daughter had been born—Becca had done the only thing she'd been able to think of: she'd made tea.

'She's only eighteen,' her mother had been saying when she'd come back in, carrying the tray.

'Well, maybe this was for the best.'

'For the best…? For the best! How can you even suggest that losing a baby is for the best!' Elspeth had demanded, rounding furiously on her startled husband.

'Dad didn't mean it that way,' Becca had soothed. 'Did you, Dad.'

'No, of course not,' her father had said, looking intensely grateful for the intervention.

'I was just thinking that, knowing our Erica, it would have been you and Becca who ended up looking after the baby,' he'd observed, with an affectionate watery smile.

His wife had given him a reassuring smile back and said

huskily, 'I know you didn't mean it, love.' She'd reached across and clasped his hand. 'I'm just thinking if we'd been stricter with her...'

And that had been the start of a predictable orgy of self-recrimination. Recrimination! Their kind, loving parents were the very last people in the world who had anything to reproach themselves over. Going over that conversation in her head made Becca ashamed that she had almost turned back when she saw the scale of this wedding she intended to crash and disrupt. Her soft lips thinned. She just hoped that plenty of people had their video cameras handy!

Head up, she pinned on a confident smile and, picking up a corsage that someone had dropped on the floor she tucked it at a jaunty angle into her buttonhole. She intended to see to it that the society wedding of the decade *didn't* go without a hitch.

CHAPTER TWO

CHRISTOS watched the irate best man vanish around the side of the building and suppressed a twinge of guilt. For a second he was tempted to follow him, but instead he blew on his fingers to revive the circulation. It struck him as faintly ludicrous that even after all that had happened his first instinct was to bail his cousin out.

What Alex needed was not someone to hold his hand and wipe his nose—he needed to take responsibility for his own actions. Christos's attempt the previous year to instil a sense of responsibility into the younger man had failed spectacularly.

When he had spelt out the new rules to his cousin, the younger man had laughed.

'This is a wind-up. You're bluffing.'

Christos had shaken his head. 'Turn up at the office more than once every six months, and when you're there do more than drink coffee and chat up female staff.'

'I delegate,' Alex had protested.

'No. *I* delegate; you sponge. Work, cousin—or the very healthy cheque that's credited to your bank account every month won't be there.'

Christos hadn't been bluffing.

There were a number of family members who had called him a heartless monster for refusing to be swayed from his decision—though naturally not to his face. Interestingly, there had been an equal number who had said, About time too!

But Alex's response to the challenge had not been what

he'd hoped. In fact it had been something he could not have predicted.

Christos had never decided if Alex had *wanted* him to find out, but there was no similar ambiguity when it came to his ex-fiancée's intentions. Melina had known Christos was coming to her flat that evening, to return the keys and pick up the laptop he'd left there.

'Don't be silly—there's no reason we can't be civilised. We have history,' Melina had said when he'd rung to say he would send someone round with the keys. 'You come, darling, and we can have a drink to the good times.'

The look of spiteful triumph in her eyes when he had walked in and found her and Alex naked on the floor, amidst a pile of discarded clothes and several empty wine bottles, had removed any lingering guilt Christos felt about ending their short-lived farcical engagement the previous week.

Mild disgust and contempt were *not* the responses a man was meant to have when he found the woman he had briefly contemplated spending the rest of his life with making love to another man!

He'd felt no desire to take violent retribution, no desire to wipe the supercilious smirk off his cousin's face—just a compelling urge to walk away from the sordid and tasteless spectacle.

And that was what he had done. He had slung the keys on the table and left. His only regret being that he had ever been insane enough to think *all right* and *workable* were thoughts a man should have as prerequisites for marriage.

Before Christos succumbed to frostbite, or to the austerity of his own grim reflections, his great-aunt, whom he had been delegated to escort, arrived. Christos heard her before he saw her. Her bony frame was swamped by several layers of motley fur, and her grey hair was crammed into an ancient shapeless hat, but her voice was not similarly fettered. It was loud and penetrating.

'It is not civilised. I shouldn't be surprised if this British weather kills me!' she was telling a fellow guest.

'I should be very surprised.'

A smile illuminated the lined, leathery face as Theodosia Carides identified the tall figure who had materialised at her side.

'So you did come,' she grunted, offering her rose-scented withered cheek for her great-nephew's respectful salute.

'Seeing you, Aunt Theodosia, makes the effort worth while.'

'Don't try your charm on me,' the old lady recommended, repressing a pleased grin as she accepted the arm her tall handsome nephew offered. 'I'm immune.'

The still-upright septuagenarian, who did not even reach his shoulder, did not see the need to lower her voice as her favourite nephew escorted her into the hushed, vaulted interior of the Cathedral.

'I thought you were in Australia, Christos?'

'I was.' Christos saw Melina, looking as stunning as ever, seated a few feet away. They nodded in a civilised manner to one another.

'Did Alex really ask you to be best man?'

'Yes, he did.'

'And you said no?'

Christos's expression didn't alter as he inclined his dark head in agreement—which, considering the mental picture of his ex, naked astride the groom, which was at that moment flickering across his retina, was no mean achievement.

'I expect you had your reasons…?'

Christos did not satisfy her curiosity. 'Can I take that for you, Aunt?' he asked, indicating the large portmanteau his elderly relative clutched.

'I am not an invalid.' Despite this sharp assertion, she

paused to catch her breath. 'I suppose you know that Andrea is saying your refusal is just another symptom of your deep-seated jealousy?'

Christos's dark brows lifted. 'Jealousy?'

The old lady nodded. 'According to her, you've always been jealous of her precious Alex.' No longer able to conceal her amusement, she gave a loud cackle of mirth and shared the joke. '*Apparently* you never lose any opportunity to belittle him and make him look foolish. Though from what I've seen he doesn't need much help—and so I told his mother. Andrea always was a very silly woman.'

'I must remember to avoid Aunt Andrea.'

'As if you care what she thinks. As if you care what *anyone* thinks.' Her expression suggested she approved of this attitude.

Christos gave one his most charming smiles. 'I care what you think, Aunt Theodosia,' he promised slickly.

The old lady dismissed the comment with a derisive snort. 'Does nobody but me care about tradition any more?' she wondered out loud. 'Nobody would even know this was a Carides wedding,' she continued, in the same disapproving bellow. 'Nobody has yet explained to me why they're not having a proper Orthodox ceremony.'

'Don't look at me, Aunt Theodosia. This wedding has nothing to do with me.' He was only here because his mother had got distressed and played the duty card. *'They'll think you don't like your cousin.'*

'I don't.'

In the event his honesty had not won him any points with his mother. She had bitterly enquired over the phone if he derived some form of malicious pleasure out of tormenting her.

'If he gets a little loud around you it's because you make him feel inadequate,' Mia Carides had explained.

On the other side of the world, Christos had given a wry

grin. *Inadequate* was one of the things a man might be excused for feeling if he found the woman he was to have married having sex with another man. Only he had never really been in love with Melina.

In truth, it had come as something of a surprise to Christos to hear the news of his own engagement!

When Melina had pulled her father to one side and whispered in his ear, Christos had had no inkling of the secret she was sharing. Not until two minutes later, when their host had called for hush and shared the news with the rest of the three hundred or so close friends who were there to celebrate the thirty years of married bliss he and his wife had enjoyed.

'I am happy to announce that my daughter and our dear friend Christos Carides are to be married.'

Christos had had no desire to humiliate the rather drunk Melina, with whom he had enjoyed a casual on-off relationship for several years, so he had smiled through the inevitable congratulations and gone home with the firm intention of ending the engagement the next day.

That had been his first mistake!

His next had been not to agree when a very shame-faced and repentant Melina had turned up the next morning, promising to set the record straight immediately. Her remorse had appeared totally genuine, and she'd obviously been mortified—so much so that he had heard himself saying, 'Why bother? We could give it a trial run.'

'Do you really think so, Christos?'

'Why not? We get on well enough, and it's not as though either of us is waiting for love at first sight.'

Contemplating life without love did not overly concern Christos. A person could not miss what they had never had. And perhaps, as Melina had claimed in one of their many arguments, he was incapable of the emotion?

'What do you mean, *nothing to do with you?* You're

head of the family, aren't you?' Aunt Theodosia demanded shrilly.

With a rueful smile Christos refocused his attention on the demanding little lady at his elbow. When jet lag eventually kicked in he was going to sleep for a week. 'A title with few benefits.'

His dry observation drew a crowing little laugh from the old lady, but she added severely, 'Don't whine, Christos. You have been blessed with brains, looks and health—not to mention a gift for making large amounts of money without breaking a sweat.'

The unsympathetic recommendation brought a smile to Christos's dark, expressive eyes. 'Sorry, Aunt,' he said, bowing his dark head meekly.

'This girl of Alex's has got a face like a horse,' she observed regretfully.

'Sally is a very nice girl,' Christos responded, a quiver in his deep voice.

It was at that moment he saw her.

He stopped dead, and didn't hear what Theodosia was saying—or, for that matter, anything else. She was framed in the doorway, her hair as she entered the Gothic candlelit Cathedral an incredible burnished beacon.

For a few seconds things got *seriously* surreal. But there was in all probability some perfectly prosaic reason for the rest of the world receding, leaving him with the impression that he and the redhead were the only two people in the place.

Christos, his jaw clenched, blinked hard, and the hum of conversation gradually filtered back into his consciousness. Jet lag, he concluded, loosening the constricting tie around his neck a little as he narrowed his gaze on the bright head of the slim, simply dressed woman.

He had never seen her before. Not that this made her exceptional. There were any number of people attending the wedding that he had never laid eyes on before. But, unlike this late arrival, those strangers had no connection with the prickle on the back of his neck. The groove between his dark, strongly delineated black brows deepened as he lifted a hand to the affected area.

With a first-class degree in pure maths, and the owner of a mind that was widely held to be brilliantly analytical and logical, he saw nothing contradictory in trusting his instincts. And there was absolutely no doubt in his mind that the slender redhead represented trouble of a major variety.

Perhaps the danger she represented appealed to him? Could that alone account for his suddenly out-of-control libido? He didn't have a clue, and he was not in a mood to analyse his motivation, he just knew he was going to make sure—even at the risk of major disappointment—of meeting her.

At some level he recognised that even the recent months of self-enforced abstinence didn't totally explain away the compulsion that made him unable to take his eyes off her for fear she would vanish.

Vanish? With that hair? Not likely. His eyes moved hungrily over the mass of rich auburn curls that fell down her shapely narrow back. It was *extremely* unlikely that she would be swallowed up in the crowd, even though that was clearly her desire. A circumstance that he would investigate at a later date, when other more urgent needs, like hearing her voice, were satisfied.

Christos met many attractive, interesting women during the course of his average day, but none that had ever immobilised him with lust. But now… He trained his eyes on the redhead, who was still trying hard to blend in, and drew a deep breath. This was a temptation he had no intention of resisting.

'I don't *dislike* horses, and from what I've seen the girl has got excellent child-bearing hips.'

A thoughtful expression settled on Theodosia's lined face as she imperiously reclaimed her nephew's attention with this outrageous observation and a sharp tug on his jacket.

'Is she pregnant, I wonder? It would explain the unseemly haste. What do you think, Christos?'

With an air of resignation, and still conscious in the periphery of his vision of the redhead, he guided the outspoken old lady into her seat. 'I think I should mind my own business.'

'Not that there's anything *wrong* with a pregnant bride.'

'That is very broad-minded of you, Aunt Theodosia.'

'I'm not a prude, boy.'

Christos's thickly lashed eyes narrowed in affection. 'You do surprise me.'

'And virgins are all well and good,' she observed generously.

The redhead, he noticed, was in danger of disappearing behind a stone column. He had established, to his satisfaction, that she definitely wasn't with anyone, but she was too far away for him to tell if she wore any rings.

'I'm not aware that I know any.' In his opinion it was more important to be the last man in a woman's life, not the first, if that woman was the one you intended to spend the rest of your life with.

Theodosia chose to ignore her nephew's satiric insert beyond tapping him sharply across the knuckles with her cane. 'I hardly think you're in any position to criticise. Greek men can be so hypocritical,' she observed tartly. 'You're no saint yourself, young man. At least,' she continued, 'when you get a girl pregnant *before* you put the ring on her finger you know she's fertile.'

'That's very pragmatic of you.' He cupped the old lady's elbow as she lowered herself slowly into the pew. 'But I'm not sure,' he added in a soft aside, 'that the bride's father shares your viewpoint. Or that the modern female would enjoy being likened to a brood mare.'

Just at that moment his mother, looking flushed and breathless, appeared at his shoulder. 'Christos—I need you.' Under her breath, Mia Carides said with a fixed smile, *'Don't encourage her.'*

'What do you need me for, Mother?' Christos asked, wondering if the glorious redhead's hair was as soft and silky as it looked. A man could dream of falling asleep wrapped in that hair...

'There's a problem with security,' Mia improvised smoothly. 'Such a nuisance. I'm sorry, Aunt Theodosia, you'll have to excuse us.'

Her son responded to the urgent look with a languid smile which made his mother's diplomatic expression wobble for an instant as she clenched her teeth. Her son, as she knew, could be very vexing when he chose.

'Aunt Theodosia and I were just discussing the blushing bride, Mother.'

'I know—I heard you. So did half the guests,' Mia observed, waving graciously and bestowing a serene smile on the bride's indignant parents.

Undeterred, Aunt Theodosia continued, 'This family *needs* more babies. What is wrong with you young people nowadays? When are *you* going to have some babies, Christos?'

Christos bent and pressed his lips in a courtly gesture to the frail, age-spotted old hand. 'When I find someone with as much spunk as you.' *Or, failing that, red hair.* He blinked, wondering where that thought had come from.

The old lady tried to hide her pleased smile. 'If you do,' she predicted, 'it might well be the making of you. That other girl—what was her name?'

'Melina.'

'That was it. I didn't like her. She smiled too much.'

Across the aisle, Melina wasn't smiling at all. In fact she was looking daggers at a girl with red hair, who Christos had barely taken his eyes from.

CHAPTER THREE

'WHY do you encourage her, Christos?' his mother reproached him as she walked down the aisle.

While he lent an attentive ear to his mother, Christos continued to watch the troublesome redhead as she sat down, concealing all but the top of her fiery head from his view.

'Carl looked furious,' Mia added in a hushed tone. 'Especially as Sally *is* pregnant.'

The column was situated so that in addition to the top of her head he could see her neat feet, and as she crossed one leg over the other her ankle-length coat fell back to reveal a pair of worn denim jeans.

'What's the problem with security, Mother?'

'There isn't a problem,' Mia admitted, blissfully unaware that she didn't have her son's total attention. 'I just had to get you away from Aunt Theodosia before you made her say something else outrageous.'

Christos wondered if kissing the unknown redhead, fitting his mouth to hers and parting her moist pink lips, would be considered outrageous. If not, his fertile and overactive imagination was capable of conjuring several alternatives that almost certainly were!

Aware that he was breathing too fast, Christos made a conscious effort to slow his rapid, laboured respirations—not an easy thing to do when your head was filled with imaginings about the taste and touch of a woman.

'I doubt if anyone has ever *made* Theodosia do or say anything.'

'Your voice sounds strange, Christos,' his mother said,

reaching up and touching a cool maternal hand to his brow. 'And you're hot,' she said, shaking her head. 'I do hope you're not coming down with something. I have never considered air travel healthy.'

'Well, if I die of something airborne you will have the satisfaction of knowing it was at your instigation I flew halfway around the world to be here.'

'You,' his mother retorted tartly, 'are as bad as Theodosia.'

'Thank you. I just hope I can grow old as disgracefully as she has.'

His mother cast him a reproachful look, before pausing to be charming to someone important.

'You know, Mother, I think you're wrong about the security problem.'

Mia's eyes widened in alarm. 'There *is* a problem? What?'

'Nothing I can't handle,' Christos said, his eyes fixed on the top of that burnished head.

He began to work his way to the rear of the church. On auto-pilot, he returned the nods and smiles he received, all the time never losing sight of the redhead.

As she pulled the collar of her ankle-length coat up around her neck, to frame her face, the breath snagged in his throat. He had never seen her face before, yet somehow he felt as though he had known it all his life.

A man could only go on blaming jet lag for so long. Then he had to take responsibility himself.

A babe in arms chose that moment to cry, its whimper of complaint magnified by the building's impressive acoustics. By reflex her eyes—like every eye in the place—momentarily turned towards the ear-splitting sound.

He stood with his tall shoulders braced against a stone pillar and pondered the mild electric shock that had passed through his body as those eyes, the deepest and most shocking shade of blue he had ever encountered, had connected with his. He doubted the moment had been shared. He had the impression she hadn't even registered his presence.

The irony of being ignored was not lost on a man who was used to women pulling every trick in the book to capture his attention.

As he watched, the beautiful stranger raised a hand to her throat under the heavy overcoat, and he saw her chest lift as she exhaled and, biting her lower lip, began to stare straight ahead, an expression of rigid control and ferocious focus on her softly formed fine-boned features.

He studied the strangely familiar face at his leisure. She had the pale, lightly freckled complexion of a natural redhead. Her small nose, in profile, was gently tilted at the tip, and though her wide mouth was drawn taut by the tension that held her entire body rigid, he imagined that under normal circumstances it would be soft.

He got hot as he began to think thoughts inappropriate for the inside of a cathedral. The thoughts concerned that mouth. He not been a victim of such mindless lust since his hormones went crazy in his teens—maybe not even then.

As the place began to fill up he took the seat directly behind the redhead, positioning himself so that he could see her profile. She remained unaware of his scrutiny.

By the time Becca had finally entered the Cathedral the light-headed sensation she had been suffering for the past hour had been joined by a constant low-pitched buzz in her ears. She'd had to thrust her hands into her pockets to hide the fact they were trembling.

Worrying that she might fall into a dead faint at any moment and ruin everything had made it hard for her to maintain the confident air she had adopted, working on the theory that if she *looked* as if she belonged it might delay the inevitable moment of discovery.

She suspected all her symptoms had a lot to do with her caffeine tolerance. The fourth cup of coffee she had drunk at the motorway services to keep her alert had been a mistake. Her trembling knees had made sitting down sometime soon a priority.

She'd been looking for a likely place to wait for her moment when she'd seen one of the uniformly handsome young men who were smoothly directing guests to their seats bearing down on her, all charm and slick efficiency. She'd frozen and looked wildly from left to right. Then, taking a deep breath and pinning on a painfully bright smile, she'd begun to wave at some invisible person in the crowd, before walking purposefully in that direction.

What am I doing?

As she had slowed to let an elderly lady in an incredibly large hat pass, the full enormity of what she was about to do had hit her. It had been like running full-tilt into a brick wall. The fact was that deep down, until that moment, Becca hadn't expected to get this far.

Well, what were the odds? You just *didn't* walk uninvited into the big society wedding joining the only daughter of one of Britain's highest profile entrepreneurs to a scion of the fabulously wealthy Carides family.

The knot of anger lodged behind her breastbone had swelled as she'd thought of the family who imagined that money gave them the right to trample over the feelings of ordinary people. A person who had gone through life not hating anyone, Becca was now finding it surprisingly easy to hate anyone who carried the name of Carides.

Head down, avoiding eye contact she'd given a relieved sigh as she'd spotted an unoccupied pew, but as she'd taken her seat she'd realised why the spot had been avoided. A large stone pillar effectively blocked the view of the altar.

Becca didn't mind. She wasn't here for people to see her. They just needed to hear what she had to say.

Just cause… Her wide-spaced blue eyes grew uncharacteristically hard now, as she thought about the 'just cause' that had brought her here. To seduce, impregnate and then dump an impressionable teenage girl was despicable enough—but to do it when you were engaged to another woman…! Well, that made Alex Carides a different class of slimy rat entirely.

An expectant hush fell as the first bars of the 'Wedding March' issued from the organ. Becca stiffened and drew in air through her flared nostrils. On her lap, her fingers twisted. She took a deep breath and told herself, *You can do this.*

But can I?

An image of her sister's pale tragic face as Becca had driven her back from the hospital flashed into her head. It was enough to stiffen her resolve.

She had actually cleared her throat in preparation when the hand she had been expecting all afternoon finally fell on her shoulder.

CHAPTER FOUR

'I REALLY don't think that would be a good idea, do you?'

Good idea? Becca reflected, as the quivering tension left her body in a debilitating rush. That had never had any thing to do with this.

This had always been about standing up, if only in a small way, for Erica and for every other woman who had fallen for that slimy creep's lies. His future wife needed to know what sort of low-life she was getting married to, and the world needed to know what sort of man Alex Carides actually was.

Who am I kidding? This is about revenge—plain and simple!

The deep, interestingly accented voice, complete with sexy rasp, seemed very close to her ear as he added softly, 'I don't think you want to do this.'

Which, in conjunction with the heavy hand on her shoulder, translated as *I'll carry you kicking and screaming from the building if you try.* Becca decided to retreat with a little dignity intact.

Chin up, and looking straight ahead, Becca responded to the pressure of those fingers on her shoulder and smoothly rose from her seat, moving up the aisle and walking with little fuss through the metal-studded oak door just to her right which she hadn't even noticed was there.

Christos was conscious of a slow-burning anger that had started to smoulder the moment he had realised what she intended to do. God knows what 'just cause' she had intended to produce, but there was only one logical conclusion to draw. The woman who was going to feature strongly in his fantasies for the foreseeable future was one of Alex's cast-offs.

A cynical sneer twisted his mouth as he considered the opposite sex's inability to see beyond his cousin's winning smile and slick good looks.

The redhead had appalling taste—but she smelt very good! His eyes widened slightly as he recognised that he was angrier now than he had been when he had caught Melina with Alex.

If this wasn't jet lag he had a serious problem!

Her captor led Becca into a small ante-room. As the heavy door closed it effectively sealed them off from the sounds of the service beyond. At that moment reaction started to set in—in a big way. Her knees began to shake, closely followed by the rest of her.

'He's really not worth it, you know.'

'I know he's not…' As she spoke Becca turned her head, inhaled audibly, and added an unthinking and breathy, *'Goodness!'*

Which, under the circumstances—the circumstances being that she was inches away from the most sinfully gorgeous man she had ever seen—was quite restrained. If you were going to be caught, she reflected, you might as well be caught by someone breathtaking. And my goodness, she thought, still slightly stunned by the dark vision of brooding male perfection, he was gorgeous—and then some!

It was perhaps fortunate that the shaky hand she had lifted to her mouth stopped her saying something unconsidered.

Christos watched the colour rush to her cheeks and then fade quite dramatically away, leaving her marble-pale.

'I think you could do with some fresh air.' In his opinion that was the very least she looked as if she could do with.

Becca started, and realised that she had been staring at this stranger. Goodness knew how long she had been the prisoner of those hypnotic dark eyes and her own fascination.

She nodded awkwardly.

Her shoulders slumped as she followed the tall man with the longest eyelashes she had ever seen outside. Another minute—that was all she'd needed. She could have wept with sheer frustration. It was so unfair. Why was it that men like Alex Carides never paid the price?

Shame flooded through her. A great sister I am!

Outside, Becca sank down onto a conveniently situated bench that had been fashioned from a tree trunk. She was in no mood to appreciate its aesthetic properties as she bent forward and buried her face in her hands.

'Later, when you've had a chance to think calmly about this, you'll realise I've done you a favour.'

Becca's head jerked up. 'A *favour*?' she echoed belligerently. 'Look, I know you were only doing your job—though if you were any sort of security I wouldn't have got as far as I did,' she felt impelled to point out. 'But don't act as if your motives were altruistic.'

The tall, dark and gorgeous stranger looked startled for a moment, then gave a lop-sided sort of smile that made her undiscriminating tummy muscles quiver appreciatively.

'I was tempted to let you do it,' he admitted.

Tears of frustration sprang to her eyes. 'I wanted… wanted…'

'Calm down.'

He really was the most beautiful man she had ever seen—or even imagined! She ran the tip of her tongue across the outline of her dry lips and fixed him with a resentful glare. 'You could have looked the other way.'

'But then,' he observed, 'I'd have lost my job.'

Becca gave a distracted sigh. 'I suppose you would,' she agreed.

'Did you *really* want to stand up and make a fool of yourself like that?'

'This isn't about wanting, it's about…' She stopped and took a shuddering deep breath as she struggled to regain control. After a few moments her darkened eyes lifted to the face of the man beside her. 'Tell me, do you think it's right that he gets away with ruining someone's life?'

'I think you should consider it a narrow escape,' Christos observed drily.

Becca frowned at the platitude. 'What would you know about it?'

'I know quite a lot about Alex Carides.'

Which might, she mused, explain his expression of contempt.

'How can you work for a man like that?' The thought of being around such a creep made her skin crawl. The thought of being around any Carides full-stop made her skin crawl.

'A man has to eat.'

She flickered him an apologetic smile. 'Sorry—I didn't mean to moralise. Goodness, I'm the last person to do that.'

Her self-deprecating remark wiped all expression from his face.

Confused, Becca watched his dark, cynical gaze drop, and wondered at the almost tangible waves of tension emanating from him. 'Are you pregnant?'

Becca blinked, confused by the speed with which his manner had transformed from sympathy to frozen condemnation. As she read the distaste in his face twin circles of angry colour appeared on the apples of her pale cheeks.

'You think that I—' She bit back her hasty rejoinder. She didn't owe a total stranger any explanation—though knowing that he believed she had slept with a Carides made it hard for her to hold her tongue. 'Your boss makes a habit of getting women pregnant, does he?' she countered.

'Then there *is* a baby?' he said, looking sterner than ever.

'Not any more.'

'A termination?' he said bleakly.

Becca's voice grew husky with emotion as she corrected him. 'A miscarriage.'

The security guard drew a deep breath and, framing her face in his hands said urgently. 'What is your name?'

The peculiarity of his manner stood out as very strange in a day that had possibly been the strangest in her life.

'Your name?' he repeated.

'Becca.'

'Don't move, Becca. I'll be back.'

He didn't have the faintest idea if she had registered what he'd said. It was hard to tell from the glazed expression in her eyes if she was taking in anything much at all. He didn't like to leave her, but the strength of his feelings meant he had to act on them.

His timing was perfect. The main participants, along with the photographer, were emerging from the vestry, their symbolic signatures having been duly witnessed. They all stopped when they saw him.

Without responding to the varied greetings directed at him, Christos grabbed his cousin by the shoulders and pulled him away from his bride.

'What's wrong?'

Christos smiled, and his cousin looked alarmed. 'This is for Becca!' he said, and landed a sharp but controlled jab on the younger man's nose.

The groom yelled and clutched at his nose, blood oozing between his fingers. 'Who the hell is Becca?' he screamed indignantly. So Christos punched him again, and Alex went down.

She had moved. Cursing softly under his breath, Christos ran down a side path and saw her almost immediately.

'I told you to stay put.'

Becca looked at the long brown fingers curled around her upper arm. Until he touched her she had been feeling a lot better. Now her sensitive stomach was quivering violently. 'What do you think you're doing?' she said.

Considering the advice she had dished out on the subject to her sister, she couldn't go down the road of reacting to arbitrary and dangerous sexual attraction without being a total hypocrite!

'More to the point, what are *you* doing?' he queried suspiciously.

'Is that any of your business?' she countered frostily. 'And, thank you, but I can find my own way.' Her eyes slid to the hand on her arm, but he didn't react. 'I don't need an escort.'

'The head of security might have other ideas,' he retorted drily.

'That's not you?' Her frowning regard travelled the length of his tall lean person. No reason, of course, that he had to be the boss. He wasn't wearing a badge or anything. But he didn't act like a man who was used to obeying orders.

On the other hand it was easy to picture him issuing them, and having people fall over themselves to obey. An accusing frown settled on her upturned face.

'You act as if you are.' No matter how hard she tried, she couldn't she see him slotting into any hierarchy of command. This man didn't look like a team player to her.

'I'm new to the game,' he admitted glibly.

'Which probably explains why you're taking your duties too zealously,' she muttered. 'I've not committed a crime or anything. You've got no right to restrain me against my will. In fact,' she added, *'That—'* her nod indicated the hand on her arm '—is probably assault. Actually, I don't think there's any *probably* about it.'

He smiled, and Becca lowered her eyes as she experienced a spasm of sexual awareness that made her knees quiver. *What is it with me? You'd think I'd never seen an attractive man before!*

'Perhaps we should let the police decide?'

The silky suggestion brought her horrified gaze back to his face. 'You're joking?'

He shrugged and looked infuriatingly enigmatic.

Becca couldn't stop the quiver of doubt entering her voice as she added, 'I've told you, I've not committed a crime or anything.'

'You don't think so?'

He made no attempt to prevent her as she pulled her arm free of his grasp and folded it across her heaving chest, glaring up at him defiantly.

'I don't think. I know.'

Despite her confident assertion Becca couldn't prevent a shade of worry entering her voice as she reviewed her gate-crashing.

'Unless this is a question of one law for the rich and another for the rest of us.'

His dark eyes narrowed on her scornful face. 'You have a problem with people being wealthy?'

She lifted a hand to her aching head. 'No, I have a problem with spoilt parasites like the Carides.'

Aware of an expression in her captor's dark eyes that made her uneasy, she bit her lip to cut short this flow of bitter confidences.

'It's a little late to be discreet.'

'I really don't want to debate this with you. I just want—' She broke off and winced as the bells overhead broke into a triumphal peal. Face pale and composed, she lifted her eyes to his face. 'I just want to go home.'

'An excellent plan,' he said, falling into step beside her. Becca tilted her face and studied the hard angles and intriguing hollows of his dark, lean and exasperatingly sexy features. 'What,' she demanded, expelling a gusty sigh, 'do you think you're doing now?'

'Making sure you go home.'

'Are you going to escort me all the way to Yorkshire?'

'I'm going to stick to you until I'm sure you can't double back and wreak the destructive vengeance your soul craves.' His eyes locked with hers. 'I take it that *is* what this is about?'

'I suppose you're going to tell me revenge wouldn't make me feel better?'

'No, I wouldn't say that,' Christos responded, thinking of the groom with his bloody nose.

There were times in life when a man had to stop being cerebral and get physical—though he imagined there were a few people inside who might disagree with him at that moment. It would be a long time before he was forgiven for ruining the wedding. But it would be interesting to hear how they explained away the groom's face…

Becca pursed her lips and looked at him with mute dislike. She saw he was smiling. 'You have my word that I won't crash the reception or spoil the wedding photos.'

'Your word…' he mused, dragging a brown hand through his dark collar-length hair. 'You do see my problem there?'

Becca planted her hands on her slim hips and inhaled wrathfully. 'Are you calling me a liar?'

'Not as such. But,' he qualified, 'I do think you're not thinking straight right now.'

'Don't patronise me.' She gritted her teeth as she reflected on his comment. 'Not a liar, but mentally unbalanced. Gosh,' she observed bitterly, 'I feel better already.'

He met her angry eyes and released a low, husky laugh. Becca regarded him with growing frustration, but could see that it might be hard to remain angry with a man who possessed a laugh that warm and attractive. Fortunately she wasn't going to be within laughing distance long enough for it to become a real problem!

'Go ahead—enjoy the joke.' She gave a bleak wintry smile. 'I can see your point. What's a ruined life…? So long,' she added on a bitter quaver, 'as it isn't *your* life!'

'I know it feels like it to you now, but your life isn't ruined.'

She looked different, but she obviously wasn't. She was like any number of women who were willing to overlook the fact that his cousin was a total bastard.

Becca's electric blue eyes narrowed. She had never had the sort of fiery temper that was meant to accompany auburn hair, but his confident assertion had made her see red. As she swallowed hard, trying to contain her feelings, an image of her sister's shadowed eyes flashed into her head.

'What would you know about it?'

Jaw taut, she allowed her hostile eyes to linger on his lean face. Actually, it wasn't a conscious decision. The truth was that once she started looking she found it disturbingly hard to stop.

'You have to put this behind you.' *And I have to stop talking in platitudes.*

'I'd settle for putting *you* behind me. A long way behind me,' she muttered.

'Not going to happen,' he said, planting a hand lightly on her shoulder and directing her to the other side of an ancient gnarled yew tree that grew beside the six-feet-high wall. 'There's a side gate.'

There was. It was covered in ivy and easy to miss if you didn't know it was there. On the other side of the gate, Becca found herself in a narrow cobbled side street with expensive-looking cars parked down one side.

The dark-suited figure patrolling up and down with a walkie-talkie in his pocket spotted her immediately. He advanced, his intention clearly to intercept her—until he saw the man beside her. He nodded in a manner that could only be described as deferential, and walked on to meet them.

As the two men began to speak, Becca, staring straight ahead, walked past them. The narrow lane led to the main road, where people were waiting behind barriers for a glimpse of the bride. She had not quite lost herself in the crowd when she heard a distinctive footfall beside her.

'Look!' she snapped, swinging back. 'I'm not going to crash the reception, or scream abuse at the bride, so will you just back off?' *No, I'm going to sneak back home with my tail between my legs and tell my little sister I did nothing!* 'This has all been a massive waste of time and energy,' she admitted, her shoulders slumping with weary defeat.

'Well, most women in your situation would have contented themselves with a kiss-and-tell story in the tabloids. Though that lucrative option *is* still open to you,' he admitted.

When she didn't respond to this blatant provocation he tried another tack.

'Have you considered what would have happened if you had stood up and done your piece—dramatically stalled the wedding?'

Becca, about to walk away, swung back and blinked in owl-like confusion up at his face. 'What do you mean?'

'We are talking *stalled*, not *stopped*. The wedding would have gone ahead,' he elaborated brutally.

Becca shrugged. 'She's welcome to him.'

'Yes, every time I look at you I feel great waves of indifference.' In his experience a woman didn't travel halfway across the country because she was indifferent.

Stung by his blatant sarcasm, Becca had opened her mouth to deliver a biting retort when involuntarily her eyes dropped over the length of his lean, striking person. *Indifference*, she reflected, aware of the telling leap in her pulse-rate, would not be the most predictable response this man normally excited in the opposite sex.

'Or maybe this isn't about revenge?' he suggested softly.

His comment diverted Becca from the direction her own troubled thoughts had taken. The awful part was, he was right. She hadn't thought this thing through. And now he had forced her to do so she could see that she had almost set into motion a chain of events that would have ended up with the tabloid press camped on her sister's doorstep!

'I don't know what you mean,' she said, feeling sick when she thought of how close she'd come to making things ten times worse for Erica.

'Maybe you thought he'd take one look at you and realise that he'd made a terrible mistake—that you were the one he wanted all along.' As he watched her shake her head in angry denial he experienced a rush of anger. 'It wouldn't have happened,' he informed her harshly. *Because I wouldn't have let it happen.*

Becca took a startled step back when, without warning, he reached across and ran a long finger down the curve of her cheek. After making a moment's startled contact with his dark, strangely compelling gaze she swept her lashes down against her cheek and stayed that way until she had taken several deep, restorative breaths.

'You sound very sure,' she said, feeling normal again bar the strong urge to reach up and press her own fingers to the tingling area on her cheek.

Christos was drawn by the intense china blue of her wide eyes. It occurred to him that being forced to compare this face with that of his prospective bride might have caused even his avaricious cousin to experience a stab of regret.

A muscle in his lean cheek clenched. 'Look, maybe you *were* special.'

To Becca his shrug suggested he had lost interest in the subject. 'Are you trying to make me feel better?' she joked, her eyes hostile as she sketched a grim smile. 'Because I have to tell you you're not very good at it.'

Her observation made his lips quiver slightly. 'You're certainly not Alex's usual type.'

'Really? What do they have that I don't?'

Other than no personality? Christos thought as he grimly ticked off the attributes that normally attracted his cousin on his fingers. 'His usual types are young, low-maintenance blondes, with long legs, a lot of ambition, and virtually no talent for anything but wearing and buying clothes and spending his money.'

This cynical analysis made her eyes flash angrily. 'It sounds like you know the boss pretty well.' *And don't like him much,* she thought, but didn't add.

'Boss?'

Becca looked his curling lip and couldn't help but think he must be awfully good at what he did for any employer to put up with his disdainful manner.

'Well, isn't that what he is?' she challenged. 'Or does it hurt your macho pride to admit you're a lackey, like the rest of us?'

'And who are you in servitude to?'

'I'm a primary schoolteacher.

'I never had a teacher that looked like you.'

There was an insolent sexual quality to his appraisal that ought to have repelled her. Instead she felt a shiver of excitement slide down her spine.

'Actually,' he added, before she could respond, 'Christos Carides is the head of the company which paid for the wedding security today.'

Becca shrugged. The technicality changed nothing as far as she was concerned. 'He's a Carides.'

His dark brows lifted. 'So you tar everyone of that name with the same brush? Is that fair?'

'Don't lecture me on fairness,' she snapped back, tired of being the voice of impartial reason.

'Are you always this forthright?'

'Say what you mean—you think I'm mouthy?'

The retort drew a reluctant grin from Christos. 'You know, Alex is even more of a fool than I thought he was.'

'If that is meant to be a compliment, save it.' It was not good to start wondering how someone who looked like a sleek predator would kiss. 'I have no taste for insincerity.' *Or beautiful but predatory men,* she reminded herself.

His expression hardened. 'That sounds an odd thing for someone who has been Alex's lover to say. Insincerity is his speciality.'

The inflection in his deep voice as he said *lover* sent an odd, disturbing surge through Becca's body. 'Do you always bad-mouth your employers?'

'I thought you put no value on insincerity?'

'I do put value on good manners, however.'

'Now,' he said, 'you *do* sound like a teacher. I can see you in the classroom.' Not strictly the truth. Christos was seeing her in the bedroom!

The classroom was somewhere she really wished she had never left, Becca reflected. Perhaps she just didn't have the right genes for revenge and retribution? She had certainly made a total mess of this!

CHAPTER FIVE

To BECCA'S horror she felt her lip quiver as her eyes filled with weak tears. 'Damn, damn, *damn*!' she cursed under her breath, as she caught her wobbling lip between her teeth and sniffed.

'Come on,' he urged, taking her arm and pulling her into the doorway of a shop.

The edge of rough concern in his deep voice was tinged with impatience, and one or the other—she wasn't sure which—made Becca's eyes weakly fill all over again.

'I'm not coming anywhere with you,' she contended huskily. 'I'm going back home.' The thought of home did nothing to stem the flow of tears. 'I wish,' she added, burying her nose in a tissue, 'that I'd never left!' Before she lifted her head the hand he had extended towards her had fallen back to his side.

'Compose yourself—people are staring.'

This stern comment drew a strangled laugh from Becca. 'Of course they're staring.' Her watery gaze slid up and down the long, lean, masculine length of him and she started to laugh again.

He shook his head and looked at her as though she was demented.

She spelt it out. 'They're not staring at *me*.'

As she spoke a girl with a very short skirt and very high heels almost dislocated her neck doing a double-take. She caught Becca's eye and blushed.

'With you beside me they wouldn't be staring at me if I were stark naked.'

'Is this something you are planning to do?'

People probably always stared at him. Maybe after a lifetime of being beautiful and head-turningly sexy he didn't notice. Then again, maybe he lapped it up.

The latter possibility seemed the more likely to Becca, who had noticed that good-looking men were almost always vain.

As she looked at him it occurred to Becca that she had been a bit tough on her sister—accusing her, in the privacy of her own thoughts, at least, of being a bit of a push-over and not seeing through a love-rat. But maybe it wasn't just the glamour and slick lines Erica had fallen for. Maybe Alex also moved like a panther and oozed pheromones from every pore?

If a man who looked like this one set out to seduce her, what female would be able to resist? How many women had ever said I'm washing my hair *when he suggested jumping into bed?*

Her colour slightly heightened, Becca removed her eyes from the sensual outline of his mobile lips.

'About the only way you could be *more* conspicuous is if *you* were naked.' Then, because she didn't want him to run away with the idea that she'd been imagining him naked, she added accusingly, 'Are you Greek?'

He tipped his dark head fractionally in affirmation and looked faintly amused.

'I should have known.' Of course people like the Carides probably never left home without their own personal army.

'You don't have much of an accent.' He did have a very attractive voice, though. Seductive enough too.

'I was partly educated in America, where I have relatives.'

'That's where you learnt to be a security guard?'

'Operative,' he inserted gravely. 'We in the trade prefer the term *operative*.'

'Look, by all means defend your perimeter, or whatever—I don't care—but will you go away and leave me alone? You're going to look pretty silly if you're out here stalking me and someone's back there nicking the presents.'

'That situation is covered,' he assured her casually. 'And I can't risk you crashing the party on my watch.'

'For heaven's sake, I've already told you I'm not going to.'

'When was the last time you ate?'

Becca ignored him and fished around in her pockets for her car keys.

'I hope you're not considering driving in your condition? You are clearly not capable.'

Becca, whose thoughts had been moving along the same lines, grew defensive at the note of criticism in his tone. 'There's nothing wrong with my *condition*!' she snapped shrilly as she wiped the dampness from her cheeks. 'My condition has not a damned thing to do with you.'

Listen to the woman, said a voice in the part of his brain still functioning.

He watched as she lifted a hand to her head.

'You have a headache?'

'Headache' hardly covered the sick throbbing behind her eyes. 'No,' Becca lied, dropping her chin.

Christos surveyed the lines of strain around her soft mouth and wished he'd hit his cousin some more. *'Why...?'*

The anger in his voice brought her head up. 'Why what?'

'I suppose you think that you love him?' *They always thought that.*

Becca stared at him, then lifted her chin. 'I hate him!' she whispered.

'They say hate is closely related to love.'

'Then *they* are as stupid as you.' She delved again into her pockets, and this time produced a bunch of keys, which she jangled angrily at him. 'I've every intention of driving.'

Her brow furrowed in concentration. 'When I've remembered where I left my car.'

Above her, she heard him sigh deeply in exasperation. 'Hand them over.'

Becca looked at the long brown fingers extended towards her and blinked. 'What...?'

'Hand the keys over.'

'You make it sound as though I'm drunk and incapable!' she protested indignantly.

'You're definitely incapable.'

Why am I standing here like a spineless idiot, listening to him? 'I'm going to walk away, and there's not a thing you can do to stop me.'

'When did you last sleep or eat?'

She looked at him blankly.

'We'll buy some sandwiches on the way to pick up my car.'

'*Your* car?'

He levelled a look of impatience at her. 'Do you intend to wander around the city on foot all day, looking for your car, or do you want help?'

When he put it like that... 'All right,' she said ungraciously, then added, 'I really don't know why you're doing this.'

'That makes two of us,' he responded cryptically.

Becca looked around the luxuriously upholstered leather interior of the car with a suspicious frown. 'This is a Jaguar.'

'Call it a perk of the job,' he suggested, slinging his beautifully tailored jacket carelessly into the back seat. His tie, which he had unfastened from around his throat, rapidly joined it. After he had unfastened the top button of a pristine white shirt to reveal a discreet section of smooth brown flesh he turned the ignition.

'Some perk,' Becca muttered, pressing a hand to her wayward stomach as she concentrated on *not* noticing the shadow of body hair on his chest visible through the fine fabric of his shirt. She had noticed that the uncomfortably visceral effect this man's brand of sexuality had on her had got worse since she'd got into the car.

Which rather begged the question, *Why the hell did I get in?*

He turned his head and looked directly into her eyes and smiled. It was a sinfully sexy smile. Becca vocalised her growing irritation.

'I don't know what I'm doing here with you.'

'You can thank me later.'

'After we've found my car?'

'It's probably been clamped and towed by now,' he predicted. 'You really don't have the faintest idea where you parked?'

Becca flushed. He made it sound as though she made a habit of losing her car. 'I'd been driving all night and I ran out of petrol, and—' She stopped, her expression brightening.

'I bought a parking ticket from one of those pay-and-display things. The stub will be in my—' She looked around for her bag and her face dropped. 'Oh, no!'

'What's wrong now?' This woman, Christos decided, was a walking disaster area.

'I've left my handbag back in the Cathedral. At least,' she qualified, frowning as she mentally tried, without much success, to retrace her steps, 'I *think* I have.'

'My goodness, you really are a great loss to covert operations, aren't you?'

Becca wasn't listening. 'Everything is in it. My wallet…*everything*. Just when I thought this day could not get any worse.' She heaved a sigh. 'I have to go back.'

'Do you really think that is such a good idea?'

She turned her head to glare resentfully at him. 'You make it sound as though I have a choice in the matter. Even if I find my car, I can't get back home without money.' Her lips quivered.

Christos glanced across and saw her blink back the well of tears that made her extraordinary eyes shimmer. 'I can let you have some money,' he said, without analysing the impulse that made him want to help her.

The careless offer made her stiffen. 'You think I'd take money from a total stranger?'

One dark brow angled as his eyes swept across her indignant face. He wondered, not for the first time, how his cousin had got involved with this woman. 'You're assuming that there are strings attached to my offer?'

'No!' The groove between her brows deepened and suspicion formed in her eyes as she wrapped her arms around herself in an unconsciously protective gesture. 'Are there?'

'That is a nasty and suspicious mind you have there. You can treat it as a loan, if that makes you feel better.'

'I won't treat it as anything because—' she began, and then with a gasp broke off and yelled, 'That's my car!'

He briefly removed his eyes from the heavy flow of traffic. 'Which?'

'The blue Beetle.'

'Good grief!'

She bristled at the implied criticism. 'Meaning...?'

'Meaning they don't make them like that any more,' he inserted smoothly. 'Fasten your seat belt,' he added sharply as she began to fumble with the clasp.

Becca ignored him. 'Stop the car!' she countered.

He ignored her in return and she let out a loud wail as she saw her blue Beetle vanish from view. Hands clenched in her lap, she glared at his remote profile. 'Why didn't you stop? Didn't you hear what I said?'

'It would have been hard not to. You have a very penetrating voice. I could not slam my foot on the brakes without causing an accident.'

Her lips tightened. 'Back up, then!'

'This is a one-way street,' he informed her, without responding to her imperious instruction.

'Stop there!' she cried, indicating the empty inside lane.

'That is a bus lane. I'll get arrested.'

Becca cast him a look of extreme dislike and received an insolent half-smile in response. 'And I suppose you've never broken a rule in your life?'

She gave a derisive snort when he didn't respond. One look at him, she thought, and you could see he had been bending rules all his life.

'It wouldn't surprise me if you've got a criminal record a mile long!' she contended crankily. 'Just let me out here and I'll walk back.'

'It is snowing.'

'I'm aware that it is snowing.'

'If I stop the car are you so sure you can locate your car again?'

'Of course I can locate my car.'

'Well, so far you've not displayed even the most rudimentary sense of direction. If you will try to control your impatience I'll get you back to your car. Also,' he added, sliding her a sideways glance, 'throwing yourself from a moving car is not going to help.'

'I'm neither stupid or suicidal,' she snapped.

'Fine—but humour me, will you? Take your hand off the door handle.'

Becca, who hadn't known she was holding it, did as he requested.

'Good girl.'

'Don't patronise me!' she flared.

'Are you always so aggressive? It is hardly feminine,' he observed disapprovingly, just before he drew his vehicle off the road and reversed into a space that Becca wouldn't have dared attempt. 'Now we will go and retrieve your car.'

Becca flung open the door. 'I don't need your assistance.' The fact that she turned and almost lost her balance on a patch of lethal black ice did not lend weight to her contention. She waited for a sarcastic comment, but it didn't come. So, chin up, she strode off.

'You're going in the wrong direction.'

The drawled comment caused Becca to close her eyes. She took two more steps before, with a sigh, she swung back and saw him standing there, his arms folded across his chest, watching her.

'Fine—you lead the way, then,' she returned grudgingly. And, as much as she longed to get back home, part of her hoped he would get lost.

He didn't.

Apparently he was one of those people who possessed an unerring sense of direction—and, not once displaying any uncertainty, moderating his long-legged stride to allow her to keep up with him, he led her back to her parked car.

Becca gave a sigh of relief when she saw it, and ran past him, repressing an urge to hug the rusty old heap. While she was inserting her key in the lock he walked around the car.

'This thing actually goes?'

'Of course it goes,' she retorted with dignity. He lifted a sceptical brow and she added awkwardly, 'Well, thanks for your help.' Frustratingly, he failed to recognise this obvious cue for him to leave.

'You are proposing to drive back home with no money?'

Becca frowned. 'I've told you…'

'Pride is all well and good.' And this woman obviously had too much of it for practical purposes. 'But how do you think you're going to get back to Yorkshire with no money?'

Becca spirits slipped another notch but stubbornly she lifted her chin and glared at him with loathing. 'How do you know I come from Yorkshire?'

'You told me. Service stations are not going to accept an IOU for petrol.'

Becca, unable to deny the accuracy of his statement, looked at the wad of notes folded in his outstretched fingers. Eyes narrowed, she turned her face up to his. 'I've told you, I can't take money from a total stranger.'

Christos gave an exasperated snort and said something incomprehensible in his native tongue.

'I don't understand a thing you're saying.' *But it sounded good when he said it. He really did have the sexiest voice she had ever heard.*

'Roughly translated, I suggested the obvious solution would seem to be for me *not* to be a stranger.'

'Where I come from people who move into the village are called outsiders even when they've lived there for twenty years—' She broke off, her eyes widening as he took her face between his big hands.

At some level she knew that she should have stepped back. There was nothing to stop her—nothing except the strange compulsion exerted by his dark gaze that overrode her natural predisposition to caution.

'What do you think you're doing?' she demanded, desperately trying to sound frosty and in control. In reality her heart was thudding fast and heavy, and she had rarely felt *less* in control in her life.

The question was echoed in Christos's head, but he ignored it. Her skin was so soft. Fascination gleamed in his dark eyes as his thumb explored the smooth contours of her flushed cheek.

Her eyes flew open as he fitted his lips to hers. *How had she known they would be a perfect fit?* Then, as his sensual mouth moved against hers, Becca's lips parted and she groaned with helpless pleasure into his mouth. She lost all sense of self-awareness as he skilfully plundered the warm recesses.

It was only when he'd stopped kissing her, and she was trying to breathe again that Becca realised her fingers were laced into his dark hair. Swallowing and biting her lips, she untangled her fingers, muttering, 'Sorry…' over and over, like a total moron.

She was shaken to the core by her response; significant areas of her overheated body still throbbed with the after-effects.

Deliberately not looking at his face but directing her stare straight ahead backfired spectacularly—straight ahead was his chest.

And his chest set in motion a train of thought that began with recalling how incredible it had felt to be held against his lean hard body. It ended with her going weak with sheer longing as she remembered the intimate pressure of his erection grinding into her belly through the layers of clothing that separated them.

'Right, so now we are no longer strangers.'

Her dazed eyes lifted at this throaty observation. 'We're not…?' Personally she had never felt stranger in her life.

'At least where I come from we're not.'

It was some comfort that he looked slightly less assured than normal.

He took her wrist and unfurled her fingers. 'So now you can take this in good conscience.'

Becca looked blankly at the money he'd pushed into her hand, then back at him as her cheeks began to burn in shame.

'I'll return it,' she said, taking one last look at his lean, dark face through the sweep of her lashes.

She took the money—not because she was concerned about how she was going to get home, but because it was easier to take it and run than examine what had just happened.

She flung the money on the front seat and belted herself into the Beetle. Crunching the gears atrociously, she drove away without a backward glance. It wasn't until she had gone a mile that she realised she had no idea what his name was or where she should return the money to.

CHAPTER SIX

THE snow got steadily thicker. Becca had spent a couple of worrying miles wondering if it would be better to stop when the decision was taken out of her hands. The engine cut out and, despite repeated attempts, she failed to revive it.

What to do now? Sit tight, or walk for help?

That decision too was almost immediately taken out of her hands when her door was flung open and the tall dark stranger snapped.

'Come on.'

'What are you doing here?' she gasped.

'Saving you. But you can say thank you later.'

Becca's thought were racing. 'Were you following me?'

He poked his snow-covered head inside, clenched his teeth and grinned—and things inside Becca clenched too as mindless desire clutched low in her belly.

'No, I just happened to be passing.' He rolled his eyes and clicked the catch on her seat belt. 'Of course I was following you!' he yelled, his voice very loud in the confined space. 'Now, come on—before my car gets snowed in too.'

Stepping out into the snow, she felt the wind steal her breath for a moment. He grabbed her hand and yelled above the wind. 'Come on!' He drew her towards the Jaguar that he had pulled up just behind her Beetle.

Sitting in the warmth and comfort of his car, with snow melting on her face and hair, she watched him turn the ignition.

'Why did you follow me?'

His eyes swivelled towards her and he said, without any discernible change of expression, 'I wanted to kiss you again.'

Of course this was the cue for her stomach to take a dramatic dive and her temperature to rise by several degrees.

Obviously he was joking. 'It wasn't that good a kiss.'

This time when he looked at her his eyes held a raw, hungry gleam. 'Oh, yes,' he said, his eyes dropping to her mouth, 'it was.'

Their journey to a country house hotel a couple of miles back was completed in total silence.

'Where's this?' she said, looking at the black-and white-timbered Tudor Inn while she thought about how good his mouth had felt.

'Hopefully where we're spending the night. You have a problem with that?' he asked, angling a dark-eyed, questioning look at her face.

Becca read the question in his eyes and her heart skipped a beat. A sharp thrill of excitement slid through her body, bringing a flush to her cheeks and a feverish glitter to her deep blue wide-spaced eyes.

'It would probably be dangerous to try and drive any further.'

'But not impossible,' he admitted, making it difficult for her to pretend even to herself that this was anything other than what it was.

Do I know what I'm doing? God, yes. I'm playing with fire.

'We need a room.'

She snatched an uneven breath and thought, *I need my head tested.* Deep inside the liquid excitement low in her belly tightened another painful notch.

'Two rooms.'

'That seem a little excessive, but if that is what you want.'

His expression suggested that he knew perfectly well it wasn't what she wanted at all.

'One thing,' she said, catching hold of his arm as he was about to step out of the car.

'What?'

'What's your name?'

He grinned. 'I'm Christos, *yineka mou*.'

The Tudor Inn turned out to be half empty, several guests having been unable to make it because of the weather. When he heard where they had come from the proprietor expressed surprise that they had risked the drive.

He asked if they wanted a meal and Becca, with visions of candlelight, open fires, long, awkward silences and her companion's sexy eyes, said quickly, 'No—just some sandwiches, if that's all right.'

The man behind the reception desk looked at Christos, who said that sandwiches would suit him too.

'Fine. I'll leave them in the snug and you can have them when it suits you. There'll be a pot of coffee there too—just help yourselves. Up the stairs, the first two rooms on the left,' he said, handing Christos the keys.

'Nice man,' Becca said as he left.

'I could be nicer if you'd let me,' Christos said, not looking at her.

Becca was so startled that she didn't know whether to slap his face or say, *Prove it.*

The fact she had even considered the latter said a lot for her state of mind! She turned her head, expecting to see a satirical glint in his eyes or a mocking smile on his expressive lips. She was rendered breathless by the expression of driven need stamped on his dark, lean features.

Breathless she could cope with. The excitement that

swirled through her veins like a powerful narcotic was another matter.

'I'm sure that modesty is one of your most charming traits,' she said, trying for detached and faintly amused and failing horribly on both counts.

'You are ready to go up?'

Becca shook her head and pressed a hand to her throat, where she could feel a revealing pulse throbbing. She walked towards the fire blazing in the inglenook. 'I'll explore a little down here first.'

Christos nodded curtly but didn't say anything.

Becca waited five minutes and then went up. She had no problem locating the rooms the landlord had mentioned, but the question was which one Christos had taken. With no regard for security he had left both sets of keys in their corresponding locks.

Taking a deep breath, she opened the first door. The room was empty. She closed it quietly, careful to make no sound, and stepped back out into the hallway. Trembling a little, she opened the second door. The carefully prepared expression of surprise faded from her face as she stepped into the room. This room too appeared empty.

The sense of anticlimax was intense.

'Done exploring?'

Becca jumped like a startled deer and spun around. Christos stood in the doorway of the *en suite* bathroom. The moisture clinging to his golden skin and the towel looped about his waist suggested he had just that moment stepped out of the shower.

Becca stood nailed to the spot by sexual longing as she took in the details of his lean, streamlined body.

He was quite unbelievably gorgeous, she decided, as her eyes greedily explored the perfect definition of his flat belly, broad chest, and long, muscular thighs. He had the toned body of an athlete—though she could honestly say that she had never looked at an athlete with a flat stomach and imagined running her tongue across it!

The simmering silence stretched and stretched.

'I just…the door… This is your room. I'm sorry—' Her disjointed sentence faded away to nothing as she lifted her hands to her hot cheeks. 'I'll go,' she added, shaking her head.

'*No!*'

She turned.

A muscle along his jaw clenched. 'Don't go, Becca.' The lashes lifted from his cheeks and Becca gasped. Looking into his molten eyes made her dizzy with desire.

'Stay with me.'

Before the throaty plea had left his lips a needy moan had left her own and she was running towards him.

She felt relief as his strong arms closed around her, holding her so tight she couldn't breathe. He kissed her again and again, with a driving desperation. Becca didn't want to care about breathing, she just wanted this not to stop any time soon. She wanted to carry on feeling like this for ever. It was insane and she loved it.

This isn't love, it's sex, she told herself, and then thought, *Why give it a name? It's just incredible—and so is he.* Then she stopped thinking, because she was too busy *feeling!*

Still kissing her, Christos slid the coat from her shoulders, then peeled away her jumper. 'I have thought about taking off your clothes from the very second I saw you. Have you any idea how good you smell?'

He unclipped her bra, and as he cupped one breast in his hand rasped, 'You're totally perfect.' He picked her up and carried her to the bed.

Becca lay there, and realised that this was the first time in her entire life she had actually surrendered control. She had had no idea that it could be such a spectacularly liberating experience. The glorious contradiction made her laugh, and then she stopped, because Christos was unfastening the towel from his waist. She gave a fractured gasp as her hot, hungry eyes slid down his sleek hard body.

'Oh, my…' she whispered as he arranged his long length beside her. She touched his skin. It was like warm silk and still damp from his shower. 'I want to touch you.' As she looked at him the intimate ache between her thighs became an insistent throb.

Christos held her eyes as she laid a hand on his belly, letting one finger trail downwards, then he groaned and, leaning over, fitted his mouth to hers.

Becca's hands slid into his hair as they kissed. He touched her everywhere, his clever hands gliding over her skin. Becca groaned, feeling his cool fingers on her hot flesh, and writhed with pleasure, begging him in a husky, broken whisper not to stop.

'I won't,' he promised, pressing damp, hot kisses to her neck and eyelids before plunging into the sweet moisture of her mouth.

When he slid down her snug-fitting jeans she wriggled her hips, arching her back and lifting her bottom off the bed to help him.

She had no control over the keening cry of pleasure that was drawn from her throat as his hand slid between her thighs. 'You are *very* good at this!'

'You like this too?' he asked.

Watching his dark head as he licked his way down her stomach was the most mind-blowingly erotic thing she could have imagined. Becca could do little more than moan as she gave herself over entirely to the deep tremors of burning pleasure that passed through her body as he continued to caress her with skilled hands and lips.

When he finally parted her thighs and settled between them she entered a place she had never been before. She was beyond sanity. She just knew that if he didn't take her now she would die.

She screamed something to that effect and dug her nails in his back. In the moment before he thrust all the way into her, hard and hot, she closed her eyes, preserving for ever in her memory the image of his face drawn taut into a mask of raw and primitive need.

As he drove into her she gave a shocked little gasp and whispered *yes* against the damp skin of his neck. She dug her nails into the firm smooth skin of his shoulders. Said *yes* again as she caught the rhythm.

'Look at me!' he said thickly, and she did—just as it hit her so fast and strong that she stopped breathing. Muscles tightened, nerve-endings throbbed, all in perfect blissful, mind-blowing harmony.

Inside her she felt the heat of his pulsing release and her arms wrapped tight about him, wanting to prolong this moment for ever.

For a long time they just lay there, with his face turned into her neck, their sweat-slick bodies entwined, but finally he rolled away and gave her a sleepy, heartbreakingly gorgeous smile.

'I was tired. Next time it'll be better.'

'Then next time I will die,' she responded with total conviction. There was only so much pleasure a body could take.

Pulling her into his arms, he laughed huskily and fell almost immediately asleep.

CHAPTER SEVEN

SITTING amidst the raw ingredients that would become a Bronze Age village for Year Four's history project, despite all her best efforts Becca found it hard to concentrate on the challenge of inspiring enquiring young minds.

Christos's dark, lean face kept creeping into her head. That and a feeling of profound loss and misery—which was ridiculous, because you couldn't lose something you had never had in the first place.

Ridiculous or not, she was unwilling to release the image. Dwelling on the impossible perfection of his sensual mouth made her tummy muscles quiver, and recalling the depth of emotions his dark eyes were capable of communicating sent a jolt of neat sexual longing through her body.

She looked at her trembling outstretched hand and bit her lip. *Face it, while you're obsessing about him he's probably staring into his gorgeous fiancée's eyes. Or, more likely,* she reflected, *unscrewing a pot of glue with unwanted violence, her cleavage!*

She felt a tear of anger and misery slide slowly down her cheek and lifted a hand to blot it.

This has to stop, she told herself sternly.

For heaven's sake, anyone would think I'd fallen in love with the man! She froze and sucked in her breath... *Oh, my God...!*

She could only ignore what was so glaringly obvious for just so long, and Becca knew that her period of blissful ignorance had just come to an end. For the past months, while she'd been congratulating herself on her practicality, on her ability to face her problems head-on and come up with solutions, she had been asking the wrong questions!

This wasn't about maternity leave and childcare. This wasn't about how a dedicated single parent could make a good job of bringing up a child. This was about coming to terms with living without the man she loved.

It was stupid, no doubt about it. Criminally insane, almost certainly. But she had fallen for a man who probably didn't even remember her name!

Becca let out a strangled laugh. Maybe his PA still had it on file somewhere? Her lips twisted as she recalled the terse, typewritten note that had accompanied her lost bag when it had arrived by courier. Angrily she brushed away the tears that were flowing freely down her cheeks. It had been the sheer formality of the card that had hurt the most.

Would it have killed him to sign his own name? Even a one-night stand should be afforded that courtesy.

Instead Christos had delegated the task to one of his darned minions. After viciously tearing the note to shreds, and indulging in a crying jag that had left her face red and blotchy, Becca had reassembled the pieces and jotted down the address.

She had felt slightly better when she had shoved the sum of money she'd been forced to borrow from him into an envelope and posted it. *Closure* she had defiantly termed her action. But she hadn't yet realised that she was pregnant.

Anchoring her hair from her face, she got to her feet and caught sight of herself in the mirror.

'I'm an idiot,' she told her teary reflection. 'Only an idiot would fall in love with the enemy.' Then, as the room tilted without warning, she sank back down onto her knees and let her head flop forward.

She was back there—back in that room, at the moment

she had discovered the identity of the man who had just made love to her.

Getting out of bed by the light of the moon that had filtered through the half-closed curtains, her intention to get a glass of water, instead she had tripped on his discarded trousers. As she'd picked them up his wallet had fallen from the pocket. Dropping to her knees, she had retrieved a credit card that had spilled out.

She'd been about to slide it back in when the name had leapt out at her.

She'd frozen, an expression of horror stealing over her face, then she'd risen to her feet and gazed at the sleeping figure. *Oh, no. What have I done?*

She had gone to the bathroom, barely registering what she was doing as she'd pulled on her clothes in the dark. Going back into the bedroom, she had actually got as far as the door when a compulsion she hadn't been able to resist made her walk across the room to the bed where Christos lay.

In the half-light she'd seen his chest rise and fall, slowly and rhythmically. The sheet gathered low on his hips had revealed his lean, tightly muscled torso. His skin, warm and smooth, had invited her touch.

She could remember the tight feeling in her chest that had forced her to breathe shallow and fast, to drag enough air into her lungs, as she'd sunk to her knees beside the bed and stretched out her hand.

Her fingertips had tingled as they'd hovered a whisper away from his skin. A deep, voluptuous sigh had escaped her aching throat as her fingers had made contact with his bare flesh. She'd allowed her sensitised fingertip to draw a line down his flat belly, feeling the shift of muscle under the satiny, slightly damp skin.

She should have run then, when he had stirred and murmured throatily in his sleep, but the feeling had been addictive.

But Christos had opened his eyes and she'd no longer had that option. For a moment he'd looked at her blankly, then recognition had spread across his face and warmth and passion had stirred hotly in his eyes.

He had reached for her, touching a strand of bright hair, then seen the dampness on her face and pulled himself upright, dragging a hand through his tousled dark hair as he'd flicked on the bedside lamp.

Becca had blinked in the brightness.

'You're crying.' His thumb had brushed a shiny tear from her cheek.

Becca had closed her eyes, the tenderness and concern in his deep voice making it hard to cling to her righteous anger and disgust.

'You're dressed!'

She'd opened her eyes in time to see him swing his legs over the edge of the bed, apparently oblivious to his naked state. Becca hadn't been. She'd been a long way from oblivious. There was not an ounce of surplus flesh on his long, lean body to conceal the ripple of taut, perfectly formed muscle as he moved.

As he'd taken her face between his hands her lashes had lifted from her cheeks, their eyes had connected and a visible quiver had run through her body. Even knowing the warmth in his dark eyes was fake, that he was not, in fact, sensitive and caring, but a manipulative, lying rat, she'd had to struggle against her gut reaction.

A gut reaction that had said *This is a man you can trust with your life*. Were her instincts wrong this time!

'What is wrong, *yineka mou*?'

The endearment pierced her like an arrow aimed at her heart. 'I've never had a one-night stand in my life before.'

And what a time to start! 'I don't care if you don't believe me,' she added defiantly.

His response was immediate. 'Of course I believe you.'

She leaned back on her heels and his hands fell away. He watched, perplexed and concerned, as she covered her face with her hands.

'Becca!' he exclaimed, oozing the sort of the caressing amusement she found almost impossible not to respond to. 'You don't think I'm the sort of man who has double standards about such things, do you?' He took her wrists and drew her hands from her face. *'Do you?'*

Incapable of responding, Becca just looked back at him, thinking even at that moment, when she hated him, that she had never in her life seen anything as beautiful as this despicable man.

'I'm the last person in the world to judge.'

Becca, who was busy judging herself, bit down hard on her lip, and felt her eyes fill with angry self-recriminating tears when she heard him say, 'Besides, this wasn't a one-night stand.'

Becca knew she shouldn't even respond to such a ludicrous contention, but then this had been a night for doing things she shouldn't have!

'You mean there are going to be more nights like this?' Without allowing him time to respond to this angry question, she gave a bitter laugh and added, 'Well, there couldn't be, could there?' she reasoned.

'There couldn't?'

The indulgence in his tone made her want to scream. 'Even someone as s…stupid as me, Christos—' she heard the self-pitying quiver in her voice and lifted her chin in angry defiance '—is eventually going to catch on to the fact you're not a sexy security guard.'

She saw him stiffen and gave a triumphant little smile,

even though she'd never felt less triumphant in her life. She felt sick, used, and deeply ashamed of herself.

'Yes. I know that you're really a Carides.'

'Ah...'

Her voice rose to an accusing shriek as she yelled, 'Is that all you've got to say?'

His glance moved to his wallet, lying on floor where she had dropped it. She met his eyes and produced a disdainful sniff.

'Well, I suppose I should thank you. Not every girl can say they've slept with a Greek tycoon. *Tycoon*—is that the right term?'

'Somewhat generic, but it is one that has been used before,' he admitted, studying her flushed, tear-stained face. 'Don't you think you're overreacting slightly?'

'Overreacting?'

'Essentially nothing has changed. I am the same man I was an hour ago.'

'If you really think that you're insane.' Her hands balled into tight fists as she rasped in a low, driven voice, 'I'll never, *never* forgive myself for sleeping with the enemy.'

He looked startled. 'Enemy?' he repeated slowly. 'Is that what I am now?'

She met his eyes. 'You always were. I just didn't know it.' Her eyes were filled with bitter tears of self-recrimination as she lifted her head.

The golden skin of his face pulled taut against the carved contours of his darkly handsome face as he watched her. 'And you would condemn me because of my name?' he wanted to know.

'No, I condemn you by your actions—which, not to put too fine a point on it, *stink*! What's wrong?' she asked. 'Can't you get a girl into bed without lying through your teeth?'

The anger that she sensed had been building in him

seemed to drain at her jeering insult. 'My name doesn't normally act as such a hindrance when it comes to attracting the opposite sex.'

The horrid image of hordes of nubile babes all competing for his favours did not do much to improve Becca's state of mind.

'Well, I'm not so easily impressed by your money. And quite frankly,' she confided truthfully, 'the sound of your name makes me feel physically sick!'

'You would judge me by my cousin's standards?'

'As far as I can see, you're two of a kind,' she retorted, and had the satisfaction of seeing the flare of furious anger in his eyes before he vented a violent-sounding foreign expletive.

'I can understand that, after what he has done to you—'

'Not me. My sister,' she inserted, unable to meet his devouring eyes without her stomach taking a violent, quivering nosedive.

Becca endured the stunned silence that greeted her words for a full thirty seconds before her control crumbled.

'For pity's sake,' she entreated, averting her gaze and covering her hot cheeks with her hands. 'Will you put on some clothes? *P…please?*'

Christos gave no sign of having heard her fractured plea. 'You mean you and Alex never—?'

'I've never been introduced to the man,' she cut in. 'Well, I've seen him at a distance,' compulsive honesty compelled her to admit, with scrupulous accuracy. 'Dark, very little chin to speak of, and,' she added, frowning in distaste as she recalled, 'a loud voice. Not really my type.'

Christos's normally rich, expressive voice acquired a dull monotone as he tersely interrogated her. 'You haven't slept with my cousin?'

Dragging her wandering eyes back to his face, she achieved a passable shrug.

'You were never carrying his child?'

'I've never slept with a Carides before tonight.' Her eyes slid down his lean, toned body, gleaming in the subdued light, and a shiver ran through her body.

'You led me to believe that you—'

'I didn't set out to deceive you,' she cut in.

'Then as I did not set out to deceive you. We could call it quits.'

'I don't think so,' Becca retorted, shaking her head.

'We will discuss this further in the morning. Come here. You are wearing way too many clothes.'

The colour flew to Becca's cheeks. She looked at her fingers, intertwined with his, and felt despair when she couldn't summon the strength to pull free. 'You really think I'm going to come back to bed with you?'

'You're thinking about it, aren't you?' He paused and took her chin in his fingers, tilting her face up to his.

'I know you want to…you know you want to…'

A small cry of distress emerged from Becca's throat. She shook her head to dispel the lingering images and got slowly to her feet. She picked up a dry cracker from a plate on the desktop. Little and often, the doctor had advised when she had explained that she was having trouble keeping food down.

For weeks her morning sickness, which had unfortunately not been confined to the morning, had been utterly horrendous, but now things were improving.

Becca felt the familiar knot of tension in the pit of her stomach as she recognised that she couldn't delay coming clean about her prolonged bout of 'stomach flu' for much longer.

Hot tears welled up in her eyes, and she angrily dashed them away with the back of her hand. It must be due to her hormones, she decided. Certainly her emotions had never been this close to the surface before. Her hands fell to the soft mound of her belly in an instinctively protective gesture. A wobbly smile formed on her lips as a sigh shuddered through her body. Things never happened the way you anticipated they would!

The father of her child might not have had a name or face in her dreams, but one thing she had been clear about—when she told him she was carrying his child his response had been one of incredulous delight!

Something told Becca that it was never going to happen that way in real life.

CHAPTER EIGHT

THE phone ringing made Becca jump.

'Becca?'

The sound of her sister's voice made Becca smile. 'No, I'm a recording, Erica.'

'Right…yes, very funny. I was just ringing to see if you're there. And you are which is…good. See you later.'

Becca lifted the receiver from her ear as it went dead and frowned. 'Is it me?' she puzzled out loud. 'Or was that very odd?'

She had started to wonder recently if maybe her sister had guessed about the baby. Erica hadn't come right out and said anything, but on a couple of occasions she had caught her sister smiling to herself when she heard Becca blaming her recent weight loss on a bout of stomach flu.

And Erica had definitely been more understanding about her volatile mood swings than might otherwise have been expected!

She had no time to ponder the odd non-conversation with Erica, because as she put the phone down the doorbell rang. Becca glanced absently at the clock on the mantel; it was still too early to be her elderly neighbour, who often popped in after walking her dog.

Slapping her cheeks lightly, to restore a little colour to her pallid complexion, she went into the bijou hallway. Her expression set in an enquiring smile, she yanked open the door with a jerky flourish.

Her look of polite enquiry faded to slack-jawed horror as her eyes travelled up the length of her visitor—all six feet five inches of him—before connecting with a pair of mesmerising dark eyes set in a face of implacable male beauty.

For a fraction of a second Becca thought she had lost it, big-time, and was suffering from some form of hallucination. She blinked several times, but the mirage remained solid—and very real. Equally real was the great wave of enervating lust and wild longing that washed over her.

She exhaled on a big gushy sigh and grabbed the doorframe as her knees sagged.

'You shouldn't be here.'

Mixed with the fear, suspicion and disorientation she was feeling, Becca was overpoweringly conscious of an aching hunger that made her imagine putting her head against his chest and breathing in the subtle warm male fragrance of his hard body.

Shouldn't be here! It was obvious to Christos as he looked at her thin face and tired, shadowed eyes that he should have been here long before now. It was equally obvious to him that it was possible to want to wring a person's neck and protect them from even the lightest of breezes at one and the same time.

This fusion of feelings was not comfortable.

'You are going to invite me in.'

The comment was more an autocratic decree than a suggestion, and Becca, paralysed with lust and utterly terrified of what was going to come out of her mouth if she opened it again, responded by shaking her head vigorously from side to side.

His dark brows drew together as he studied her face. 'You have been crying,' he accused huskily.

At this point Becca's numbed brain finally recognised that he was inexplicably, seethingly furious! The strength of his feelings was evident in the tense lines of his coiled lean body, and underlined by the erratic muscle that clenched and relaxed like a ticking time bomb.

Becca cleared her throat and tried not to look at his mouth. Looking at his mouth made her think about fitting her own to it.

She wondered bitterly if there was some unwritten rule that only men who were very bad for you were incredible kissers.

'What was he like?' Erica had asked when, as part of her strictly expurgated version of events, Becca had explained that she had not got to confront Alex but she had bumped into his cousin, Christos.

When Becca had shrugged and looked away, to hide her blushes, her sister had added, 'I hear he's a serious hunk.'

'I suppose he is quite good-looking. If you're into all that dark, smouldering stuff.'

'Alex used to say mean things about him,' Erica had recalled. 'But thinking about it now,' she'd mused, 'I think he was actually jealous. Did you see the girl he's engaged to?'

Becca had actually felt the blood leave her face. Even though she had seen from her sister's concerned expression that her behaviour was likely to arouse suspicions, she hadn't been able to control the horror in her voice as she'd gasped, *'Christos is engaged?'*

'Oh, yes. To this stunning Greek girl. I saw her picture in that Sunday supplement.'

Feeling sick, Becca had abruptly excused herself under the pretext of making a cup of tea. When she had returned her sister had looked thoughtful, but had tactfully not commented on her elder sister's red-rimmed eyes.

Becca dragged her thoughts back to the present as an awful possibility occurred to her. 'Is she here too?' she asked, looking past Christos.

'Is who here?' Studying her expression intently, he added, 'I am quite alone, Becca.' Something that until recently had never bothered him.

As he stood to one side Becca saw a low-slung convertible parked outside her garden gate. It was about as unobtrusive as its owner! Clearly she could forget about this visit passing without notice.

Becca caught her lower lip between her teeth and suppressed a groan as she anticipated the curious questions she would be fielding from her neighbors concerning the identity of the driver of the gleaming monster for the next week at least.

Curious questions are the least of your problems, girl!

Getting him out of her head last time had been bad, so it was pretty much a given that it would be worse this time. Her eyes darkened as she recalled waking in the middle of the night, consumed with longing.

'It is cold out here.'

Becca swallowed past the constriction in her throat and continued to scan him through the dark mesh of her lowered lashes.

She had spent the last months almost convincing herself that absence had made her exaggerate his attributes. No man, she had reasoned, could be *that* good-looking. How wrong she had been!

Far from being inaccurate, the painful truth was that, no matter how true to life the mental image of him she retained in her memory, no mental image could summon up the raw sexual aura which was an integral part of him.

'There's no warm welcome waiting for you in my home, Christos.'

His mouth spasmed and a muscle in his lean cheek clenched as his dark eyes captured hers. 'This is ridiculous,' he contended.

The irritation in his husky voice brought her chin up. 'I'm extremely busy.' *Having your baby.* A tiny inarticulate gurgle escaped her lips and her eyes widened in panic. For a split second she actually thought she had said it out loud.

'We cannot have a private conversation on your doorstep.'

'I'm not about to have a conversation, private or otherwise, with you anywhere.'

'You sound like a child,' he condemned.

Becca took a deep, steadying breath and rubbed her trembling hands in a nervous gesture up and down her jogger-clad thighs. The action drew Christos's restless eyes to the soft feminine curves.

Suddenly miserably conscious that, compared to his glamorous fiancée, she must look one step removed from a bag lady, Becca wished she hadn't changed into comfy clothes when she'd got home that afternoon. Teeth clenched, she endured his narrow-eyed scrutiny. By the time his attention had moved on the tension in her body had climbed to screaming pitch.

He took his time to withdraw something from the breast pocket of his jacket. Becca, her eyes round with surprise, focused on the shiny object that swung from his fingers.

'My locket!' She reached for it and their fingertips brushed. With a tiny gasp she froze, as a shudder of sexual longing ran through her body.

Eyes downcast, she let it fall into her palm. 'Thank you.'

'We have, I think, unfinished business.'

Panic immediately engulfed her, driving every vestige of colour from her skin, as the irrational conviction that he knew about the baby gripped her.

Christos, his hand extended, stepped forward as she swayed.

Becca, unable to speak, took a deep gulp and moved her hands in a fluttery gesture to ward him off. To her relief, after a slight pause his hands fell away. But he didn't back off—a fact that Becca was overwhelmingly conscious of as she faltered.

'H...how did you know?' Half of her was actually relieved it was out in the open. The other half dreaded the recriminations that lay ahead. But at least she now had an explanation for his anger.

He gave a baffled frown, his dark brows twitching into a straight line. 'Know what?'

'Nothing.' Her eyes dropped from his. 'Just for a minute I thought…' Of course he didn't know. Nobody did except her doctor and the headmistress.

The latter had been especially supportive when they'd discussed Becca's maternity leave. She had even suggested Becca returning part-time if that suited her better after the birth.

'You thought what?'

She blinked and shook her head. 'It doesn't matter.'

'It looks to me as though it matters very much to you,' he observed, scanning her milk-pale face.

'Look…' She pinned on her best impersonal smile. 'This really isn't a very good time for me.'

His mobile lips sketched a brief cynical smile. 'I am not going away, Becca.'

'I really, *really* wish you would,' she choked.

His dark eyes narrowed on her face. 'I don't believe you.'

She gave a negligent shrug and laughed. The tinkling sound appeared to annoy him—which as far as she was concerned was a good thing.

'I can live with that.'

'You've missed me.'

The unforgivably accurate statement brought a mortified flush to her face.

'When it comes to arrogance,' she choked, 'You're in a class of your own.' *When it came to a lot of things Christos was in a class of his own.*

'There's no need to be defensive,' he soothed, as his

glance travelled over the smooth contours of her face. 'What did I say that spooked you back there?'

'I am not defensive,' she gritted back through clenched teeth. 'I was not spooked, and I do not miss you. I don't even know you!'

'True. If you did you would not resort to blatant lies.'

'So, what? Are you a mind-reader or something?' If he was she was in deep trouble.

His eyes scanned her flushed, scared face. 'I recognise the symptoms, Becca. I look in the mirror every morning,' he added, without changing expression.

'And at five-minute intervals thereafter, I expect—' Mid-crushing retort, she froze. 'What are you talking about? Recognise what symptoms?'

'Is it so impossible to imagine that I have not been able to forget you?'

Her heart was beating so fast when she managed to respond that her voice was breathy and faint. 'Quite honestly—yes.' *Outside my fantasies.* 'We had a one-night stand, Christos.'

The reminder was more for her own benefit than his. If she allowed herself to believe him she would be setting herself up for some major hurt and humiliation—which would be fine if she just had herself to consider. She ran a hand across her stomach and lifted her chin. She had the baby to think of now.

The permanently etched groove above Christos's masterful nose deepened as he retorted with chilly hauteur, 'I don't do one-night stands.'

Her temper fizzed, restoring a flush of colour to her pale cheeks. 'You're suggesting I do?'

'You owe me a goodbye.'

Becca, her brow puckered in bewilderment, shook her head. 'I don't understand.'

His eyes glittered with combustible brilliance as they

swept over her upturned features before locking down on her mouth. 'I woke and you were gone.' He swallowed and fought to contain his feelings as his voice sank to a raw rasp of outrage. 'You used me for sex and walked away.'

This last blighting accusation robbed her momentarily of the power to respond. Then she was forcibly hit by the sheer hypocrisy of his words.

'And you wanted lifelong commitment, I suppose?'

His rigid jaw tightened at the inflammatory sound of her laughter. 'It amuses you? Would you have laughed if *you* had woken and found the bed empty? Would it have been so funny then?'

'I thought you'd be relieved I'd gone. I mean the morning-afters are a bit awkward, aren't they?'

His face taut, Christos released a long fluid string of curses in his native tongue—at least they sounded like it to Becca. 'Do not be ludicrous. You know nothing about *morning-afters*… You are one of the most naïve women I have ever met.'

'So sorry if I'm too amateur for you. That I'm not *au fait* with the correct sexual etiquette for one-night stands,' she flared.

Christos gritted his teeth. 'This has nothing to do with sexual etiquette,' he growled contemptuously. 'This is about…'

About waking and reaching for someone who wasn't there. A new experience. Yes, he had been furious, and his alpha male pride had taken a body-blow, but Christos had enough self-awareness to recognise and even at some level appreciate the supreme irony.

After a lifetime of being the one to walk away, someone had walked out on Christos Carides!

And he cared. He *cared* that this woman he barely knew, with her warmth, her soft voice and softer skin, hadn't been there when he'd reached for her. No level of self-awareness was going to help him deal with that—or the fact that he had woken every morning since feeling the same way.

What would help?

'What *is* this about?' Becca asked, her voice weak.

Christos's expression lost that distant, slightly unfocused look as his eyes meshed with hers. 'Perhaps we should try it and see.'

She was almost afraid to ask. 'What do you mean?'

'I mean we should spend a night of passion and let *you* wake up alone.' He tilted his head to one side and regarded her shocked face through narrowed eyes. 'The idea doesn't appeal?'

'A night with you? Let me see…' Becca pretended to consider the idea before completing scathingly, 'That would be slightly less appealing than bubonic plague.' *Let him never know how big a lie that is.*

'You condemned my cousin for discarding your sister.'

'You're not *seriously* comparing yourself with an innocent eighteen-year-old virgin, are you?' Becca spluttered indignantly.

Dark stains of frustration appeared along the slashing curve of his cheekbones as their eyes clashed. 'You left my bed. You stole away like a thief in the night.'

Comprehension dawned in Becca's eyes. 'Sorry—I'm slow! I didn't realise why you were so hung up about this! Well don't worry—if anyone asks,' she promised, with a saccharine-sweet smile, 'I'll say *you* did the walking, so your male pride can stay intact. Not that they're likely to ask, because it's not something I'm going to boast about,' she reflected bleakly.

'Well, obviously you have told someone.' Her startled eyes flew to his face. 'Why else would your sister think it appropriate to write to me and place the blame for your fragile mental state and physical deterioration at my door?'

'My mental state isn't fragile—' She stopped as the full

import of his words hit home. 'Erica wrote to *you*?' Becca's eyes widened to their fullest extent and a dull flush of mortified colour rose up her neck until her entire face burned. Her thoughts raced. 'She knew you were coming here now?'

'I rang her to ask if you would be at home. You do realise that she is very concerned about you? She does blame me for your present condition.'

Becca barely registered what he was saying. Her thoughts were racing. It explained their odd telephone call. Erica had been checking to see if she was at home! This was nothing short of a conspiracy! What Becca couldn't understand was *why* Erica would do something like that.

'But I didn't discuss you with her—really I didn't.'

'Sometimes it is not what you say, but what you don't...'

'She shouldn't have written to you—'

Christos cut across her mortified protest. 'I had to see you anyway, to return your pendant.'

'You could have sent it with my other things. That way you could have avoided lying to your fiancée about the purpose of your visit to Yorkshire.'

Christos froze, the strong lines of his face growing taut. 'What do you know of Melina?'

'Enough to know she has my sympathy,' Becca choked.

Instead of responding to her jibe with anger, he slid his eyes from hers. This evidence of evasion confirmed Becca's suspicions.

'I despise men who cheat.' *And women who sleep with men who belong to someone else!*

'Our engagement did not work out.'

'You mean she discovered that you were a faithless bastard?'

'I mean,' he retorted, his manner abrupt, 'that we decided we did not suit. I do not wish to discuss Melina with you, Becca.'

'I don't much care *what* you wish.'

For the first time she registered that despite his definitely *not* off the peg suit, on his definitely *not* off the peg body, Christos wasn't looking his usual immaculate self. His tie was unfastened, and several buttons of his shirt had parted.

But a man who had just been dumped by his beautiful fiancée could be excused a sartorial slip or two...

'You loved her?' In her mind she saw him getting in his car and driving to forget.

Christos stared at her, his expression hard to interpret, and Becca flushed. 'It's none of my business.'

The corner of his mouth lifted, but the smile didn't reach his eyes. 'True,' he agreed.

'Did she find out about us?'

He shook his head. 'You are not the reason Melina and I are not together.'

Of course, Becca thought. I'm not important enough. Christos had just been dumped by the woman who had probably been his ideal.. maybe even the love of his life! What could have been more natural than for him to seek comfort in the first available pair of female arms?

And as I was so very available last time he probably thought... *Why not?* Well, not any more. I can't live with second best.

She lifted her chin. 'Look, you came because of something my sister wrote. But one night together hardly makes you responsible for me in any way.' Her laughter was met with stony silence. 'As you see, I'm fine.'

Becca struggled to understand his expression as he studied her in silence. The seconds ticked uncomfortably by. 'You are not fine. And I did not come because of your sister's letter.'

'Then why did you come?'

'I came because you do not belong here.'

Her nose wrinkled. 'What do you mean? Then where *do* I belong?'

His nostrils flared as smouldering velvety eyes clashed with deep blue. 'In my bed.'

CHAPTER NINE

BECCA sucked in a shaken breath and, smiling, tried to project total conviction. 'Never going to happen.'

She could avoid his eyes, but she couldn't escape the image imprinted in her mind of him lying asleep, the sheet loosely gathered around his lean hips. His chiselled features, relaxed in repose, had made him look younger, almost vulnerable.

'Why would I get back into the bed of a man who didn't even tell me his real name the first time?'

'Your outbreak of moral indignation is slightly less convincing taking into account that knowing you were sleeping with "the enemy" didn't stop you doing the same again.'

Without waiting for her to reply, he barged past her into her living room. By the time she had closed the front door and followed him he was running his finger along the spine of the paperback she had been reading.

'That's not something I'm proud of,' she said in a low, intense voice. 'And, for your information, I didn't steal away in the night. It wasn't the night, it was morning, and you were asleep. I think nothing short of an earthquake would have woken you.'

It had been two in the afternoon when Christos had woken, still jet lagged. When he'd discovered she was gone he had been consumed with anger.

'Did you even *try* and wake me?'

She turned her head and refused to answer.

'So you didn't. Why?'

'Looking at you makes me feel sick.' The childish retort made her wince, but what was she supposed to say? That

83

she was ashamed that she had made love with a member of the detestable Carides family, not once but twice? And even more shamed that she knew she would not have had the strength to say no to a repeat performance if she had waited for him to wake?

'From what your sister tells me, you've been doing a lot of that just lately.'

'Erica exaggerates.' The colour fled her cheeks as she avoided meeting his eyes. *He can't know. He can't know.* 'Stomach flu,' she muttered. 'I've had stomach flu.'

'You are well now?'

His searching scrutiny made her feel vulnerable and exposed. 'Your concern touches me, it really does.'

'I am not stupid, Becca.'

Becca covered her mouth with her hand and mumbled, 'I don't know what you're talking about.' She had doubts about denial being the best form of defence, but at that moment she had nothing else to fall back on.

'I think you do.'

She looked into his dark, lean face and recognised that denial wasn't going to work. He's relentless, she thought, in the second before the buzzing in her ears became a dull roar and the world started to tilt.

She heard him release a string of curses in his own tongue as he pushed her down into the nearest armchair.

She didn't have the strength or the will-power—never a lot of that around Christos—to struggle as he urged her head down between her knees with the terse instruction to take some deep breaths.

'You need a doctor.'

'The only thing I need is for you not to be here,' she retorted, trying to marshal her defences. The very last thing she wanted was her doctor arriving and saying that a pregnant woman needed to take care of herself.

A few moments later the world stopped spinning quite so wildly and Becca woozily lifted her head.

Christos's hand immediately fell away. In a fluid motion he rose from his squatting position and took a step backwards. Standing with his arms folded across his chest, his expression was brooding and sombre as he studied her face.

Becca lifted her head and saw lines of strain on his face that she had not noticed earlier. Sighing, she passed a hand across her eyes and apologised.

'Sorry about that—no lunch.' Her smile was painfully forced.

'We had sex with no protection.'

This blunt comment sent the colour flying back to her pale cheeks. She pressed a hand to her chest and struggled for a semblance of composure as she felt herself immersed in the sensual fog of sexual recall.

She gave a careless shrug, relieved that she had unexpected acting abilities, and blissfully unaware that she had been staring at him with silent longing for a full thirty seconds.

'The relevance being…?'

She watched the muscles in his long brown throat work as he swallowed before replying, 'Pregnant women faint.'

'I didn't faint.'

His lip curled in a sardonic smile. 'If I had my doubts before, I no longer do. You are a very bad liar. When your sister mentioned your sickness it did cross my mind,' he admitted.

She knew a scornful laugh should be her response, but Becca could only stare at him in horror. 'That's a pretty big leap to make.'

'I believe in following my gut instincts. The first time I saw you I knew—'

'The first time you saw me you knew what?' she prompted, watching as he walked across the room and picked up a pile of exercise books balanced on the arm of a chair. He pushed them onto the floor before lowering his long, lean frame onto the overstuffed floral armchair.

'That's my marking!' she exclaimed in protest. 'It's all mixed up now!' Their eyes met and she was no longer able to pretend an interest in her essays on what Year Four had done during half-term. 'The first time you saw me?' she prompted again, huskily. 'What did you know?' She despised herself for asking.

'I knew you were trouble.' His dark eyes brushed her bright hair and travelled lower, lingering on the full curve of her lips. 'My instincts are generally right.'

His eyes captured hers, and the heat she saw smouldering in them drew a tiny gasp from Becca's raw, aching throat. Fighting the sexual tension that was crackling between them, Becca nervously ran her tongue across her lips, inadvertently drawing his attention to the soft pink outline.

'Pity for us both that you didn't listen to your instincts,' she retorted thickly as his eyes darkened.

'Do you not think I've asked myself why I didn't on more than one occasion?'

'And what are your infallible instincts telling you now? No—I really don't want to know,' she said hastily.

'They are telling me you are pregnant. Are you pregnant, Becca?'

'If I am I don't see that it's any of your business.'

Anger tightened his patrician features as he looked at her with incredulous astonishment. 'If I could be the father it's very much my business,' he retorted grimly.

His comment ignited an inexplicable flame of fury in Becca, who leapt to her feet, her hands clenched and her eyes blazing. '*If?*' she yelled. '*If?* Who else would the father be if not you?'

One brow elevated, and his expression was totally unreadable as his dark, heavily lashed eyes swept across her face. 'So you *are* pregnant?'

After a short pause Becca nodded.

Christos held her eyes for a moment, then, cursing in his native tongue, clutched his head in his hands.

Becca knew that it was foolish to allow herself to be hurt by his reaction, but she had no control over the aching pain of loss she felt.

The problem was, a girl had no control over her dreams—and Becca had foolishly allowed herself to dream. She hadn't acknowledged, not even to herself until that moment, that there was a part of her that had still secretly expected him to react like a joyous expectant father.

'Are you okay?'

Her hesitant enquiry brought his head up. He looked at her incredulously, one dark brow arched. 'Me? Am *I* okay?'

She nodded. No wonder he looked gutted—he probably thought she was going to use the baby as leverage.

It was only natural really, she conceded, that if you were Christos Carides there would be any number of women who would like to trap you into marriage. Well, on that score at least she could put his mind at rest. A marriage of convenience was not on her list of things to do with the rest of her life!

'You don't have to worry, you know.'

'I don't?'

Becca shook her head vigorously. 'I've no ambition to be the next Mrs Carides.' She gave a little laugh.

'That is unfortunate. But I'm sure you will adapt.'

'What did you say?' she whispered.

He continued as though she hadn't spoken. 'I will need to rearrange my diary, but I think a wedding in four weeks' time will be possible. And you?'

'Me?' she echoed blankly.

He looked mildly irritated by her inattention. 'Will four

weeks be sufficient for you to organise things at your end? You need not worry about the actual ceremony—I will deal with those arrangements.'

'You mean you'll delegate the task?' She skidded to an abrupt halt and gave a high laugh that she managed to cut off before it tipped over into outright hysteria. She had been about to embark on a squabble about who was to arrange a marriage that was never going to happen.

Christos slanted her a frowning look of enquiry. 'What is so funny?'

'I was just thinking that insanity must be catching.' Her response caused his frown to deepen. 'You actually expect me to marry you in four weeks' time?' Strange. To look at him nobody would suspect he was stark, staring *crazy*.

'As I said, I can be reasonably flexible.'

'You? Flexible?' She gave another laugh. 'That, I suspect, will be a first.'

'I do feel that for obvious reasons—' his glance strayed meaningfully to her stomach '—sooner would be better than later.'

'Don't you, Becca?' he prompted, when she didn't respond.

'Never would be a lot better.'

'I do not think the occasion warrants such flippancy,' he reproached her.

'You think I'm flippant? Let me tell you, Christos, I'm that far away…' she held her finger and forefinger a whisper apart to illustrate her point '…that far away from having total hysterics.' She sucked in a deep breath and made a mammoth effort to stay calm. 'Let me explain this to you— as you obviously don't inhabit the same world as the rest of us. It is the twenty-first century. People don't go around getting married because they're pregnant.'

She watched his lips twist in a derisive smile. 'I have not the faintest interest in what *people* do.'

With most men the arrogant announcement would have been made for effect. With Christos, she realised with a sinking heart, it was simply a statement of fact.

'Let me rephrase that. *I'm* not going to get married because I'm pregnant.'

He heard her out patiently, while looking as though he was fighting an urge to strangle her. 'Once you've considered the situation sensibly—'

Becca struggled to hold on to her temper. 'Do not patronise me, Christos.'

He was unable to stop his exasperation showing as he went on, 'I feel sure I can rely on your good sense—'

Becca's low-pitched squeal of sheer frustration cut across his words. 'You're forgetting I don't have good sense. If I did I wouldn't be in this situation to begin with.'

'You're emotional,' he condemned.

Her eyes opened to their widest. 'Too right I'm emotional!'

'Be calm. It cannot be good for the baby or for you to get stressed.'

Becca's hands went automatically to her stomach. His eyes followed the instinctively protective gesture. 'If you don't want me to be stressed, then please go away.'

'It doesn't work that way, Becca.'

'I have everything organised—my maternity leave, childcare. Honestly, Christos, if you really want to be helpful and feel involved you could make a contribution to the child's education when he or she is older. University can be very expensive. I'm still paying off my own student loan.'

Christos angled a dark brow and looked at her as though she had gone mad. 'And what about the eighteen years before then? Will I be allowed to send Christmas and birthday presents?' The satiric bite of his words made Becca wince, and he relapsed into a fresh stream of low, impassioned Greek.

'I'd appreciate it if you didn't use obscenities in any language in my home,' she told him frostily.

He revealed his even white teeth in a savage, mirthless grin. 'They weren't obscenities. But only because I have iron control.'

'Well, I'm going to have to take your word on that, aren't I?' Their eyes clashed, and abruptly her anger towards him guttered. Give the man his due, he was only trying to do what he thought was his duty. 'I'm sure we can work something out if we put our heads together.'

Christos didn't look mollified by her concession.

'You think my involvement with this child would be satisfied with such a paltry gesture as paying for education? I am not a distant uncle.' His eyes dropped to her belly and his voice thickened as he added, with a hint of wonder in his voice, 'I am the father.'

Becca, who was still struggling with the stubborn image in her skull of their heads close together, snapped in a high, goaded voice, 'Yes! And I'm his mother—though no doubt you wish I wasn't. And,' she added, without pausing to draw breath, '*he* might be a *she*.' Her eyes moved over the impossibly symmetrical features of his dark face and she sighed, continuing to regard him with angry loathing as she thought, *Whichever it is, I really hope this baby looks like its father.*

'*We* are this child's parents, so of course your wishes are to be considered, but I think you're forgetting that the most important person here is the child. Is it not the duty of parents to put the needs of their child before their own selfish desires?'

'You're accusing me of being selfish?' she yelled, expelling an angry gasp and clenching her hands tightly in her lap. 'I'll *love* my baby, and that's the most important thing!' she declared, with an emotional throb in her voice.

'*Our* baby,' he corrected quietly. 'And I'm sure you will.' Becca had started to relax when he added, 'But what do you think is best for a child? To be brought up by a single parent or as part of a stable family unit? Do you think you are considering our child's best interests when you connive to deprive him of a relationship with his father?'

'I'm not conniving! I just didn't think you'd want to be involved. And as for marrying me—that's…well, quite frankly, it's ludicrous!'

'*Ludicrous?*' he echoed, looking outraged. 'You think that marrying me would be ludicrous?'

Becca, who was not allowing herself to think about what being married to him might involve, because some aspects were dangerously attractive, nodded firmly. 'Yes—ludicrous. You're really not thinking straight about this. It's understandable,' she admitted. 'You've had a shock. But imagine for one minute what your family would say.'

'I do not consult my family on how I live my life.'

Becca's feelings found release in a loud groan. 'But imagine what your mother would say.' Becca, who had seen pictures of the incredibly elegant Mia Carides in a Sunday supplement, suspected it would be something along the lines of *Pay the little gold-digger off, Christos.*

Head angled to one side, Christos studied her face. The intensity of his regard began to make Becca feel uneasy. She lifted her chin, suggesting a defiance she was far from feeling.

'Will you stop looking at me like that?'

Christos carried on looking at her, and thought about how soft her body had been in his arms, how it had felt to sink into her. It took him several seconds before he had sufficient control over his breathing to respond tersely.

'I think my mother would like you. She's been trying to marry me off for years.'

'Sure—she'd welcome me with open arms,' Becca sneered. 'The girl who trapped her precious son.'

'Let me tell you something about my parents. When they met my mother was promised to someone else—the son of a close friend of her family.'

'I'm sure your family history is fascinating, but...' Despite herself, Becca's curiosity got the better of her. 'She married your father, not this other man?'

'They were in love. And as she was carrying my father's babies at the time, it seemed the best idea.'

'Babies?'

He touched his chest and nodded. 'Me and my brother, in fact.' The shocked, round-eyed expression on Becca's face caused his sardonic grin to widen. 'Are you shocked that I was once a baby?' he wondered. 'Or is it the fact that my mother was not a virgin bride that makes you sit there with your mouth unattractively open?' The latter wasn't quite true. Her mouth, open or closed, was enough to fill a man's head with steamy fantasies.

Becca closed her mouth with an audible click. 'I'm not shocked,' she lied. 'But,' she admitted, 'I suppose I did picture you born clutching a Palm Pilot computer and asking what the dollar was doing against the yen. I didn't know you had a brother.'

'Five minutes older than me. He only lived a few minutes,' he revealed.

'That's so sad. I'm sorry.'

'Thank you, Becca. Now, would you like a church wedding?'

The soft sympathy vanished from Becca's face as she gritted her teeth. 'I keep telling you—I don't want to get married.'

'And what about your parents? What is their reaction to

your pregnancy? Will they have a problem with me as a son-in-law?'

'They will want me to be happy.'

'The implication being that I cannot make you happy? Yet I seem to recall you saying that I had given you more pleasure than you thought possible.'

Hot, mortified colour suffused her cheeks and she bit her lower lip. 'How can you be sure it was me?'

'I have a very good memory, Becca.' The taunting expression faded from his face as he added thickly, 'And besides, I would never confuse you with another woman.'

'Sure—I'm *very* special.'

It would have been oh, so easy to succumb to his husky velvet drawl. But Becca knew that if she ever forgot the inescapable fact that the only thing that set her apart from any number of other women who had shared his bed was the fact she was carrying his child, she would be in serious trouble. *And you're not now?*

'Look, we spent one night together!' she told him, dabbing the tip of her tongue to the beads of moisture that had broken out along her upper lip. 'We experienced a short-lived hormonal reaction,' she diagnosed. 'Which is hardly the most scientific thing on which to base a lifelong commitment.'

'But it's a good place to start,' he retorted and watching her flush deepen, added, 'A *very* good place. I am pleased that you share my belief that marriage is not a temporary measure, Becca. But a marriage based on *science*?' he drawled contemptuously. 'Marriage is a leap of faith. A gamble!'

Becca was genuinely appalled by the contention. Of course she knew that no marriage came with an iron-clad guarantee of success, but a *gamble*…? Such recklessness was alien to her nature.

Sure—you're so not reckless you're only carrying the baby of a man you barely know.

Ignoring the ironic voice inside her head, she countered tautly, 'You're not serious!'

'Certainly I am serious. Marriage is always a gamble.' Nothing in his manner suggested he found anything wrong with this concept. 'And it is frequently a compromise.'

A compromise as in marrying a woman because you'd accidentally impregnated her? she thought, shaking her head vigorously. 'I won't compromise. And I'm not a gambler.'

'Life is a gamble, *yineka mou.*'

She stared at him. 'Your life may be a gamble, but mine isn't. My life is planned…'

'Was getting pregnant part of this grand plan?'

Becca's spine snapped to attention. 'Are you suggesting I got pregnant deliberately?'

'No, that is not what I am suggesting. I am simply pointing out that life is no more predictable than love.'

Becca wondered if the expression that flitted across his clear-cut patrician features had anything to do with Melina, the woman he had planned to marry.

Christos had lost the love of his life. What did it matter to him now if he sacrificed his freedom for the sake of his child when he had lost his true love?

And how much freedom did he intend to lose? What would his marriage vows mean to him? She didn't have the faintest idea, she realised, her thoughts racing. He might mean it to be a civilised 'arrangement'. They would lead separate lives, but present a united front·for public consumption.

CHAPTER TEN

'OH NO!' she gasped, as a wave of faintness washed over her.

'You are ill?'

Becca opened her eyes and blinked, and discovered he was on his knees at her feet. As her head lifted his hands slid from her shoulders. Close to, she could see the lines radiating from the corners of his eyes...dark, velvety eyes, filled with concern at that moment.

I think you're the love of my life.

She shook her head. 'No, I'm fine.' Lies didn't get much bigger; she had never felt *less* fine in her life!

His critical scrutiny lasted. 'You don't look fine,' he said, taking her hand. It was icy cold. 'I think I should call a doctor.'

There was no doctor alive who could cure what ailed her! Becca gathered her scattered wits and forced a stiff little smile. 'That really won't be necessary.'

Christos remained openly sceptical as she pulled her fingers free of his and lifted her chin.

'Would you like me to call someone else? Maybe your mother?'

She shook her head and looked at him through a teary haze. 'No, don't do that.'

Her urgency caused his brows to lift.

'I haven't told them yet,' she admitted.

He digested this information in silence, then after an uncomfortable silence asked, 'Who have you told?'

'I haven't actually told anyone yet. Except my doctor,

obviously, and Gillian—the headmistress where I work,' she explained. 'Oh, and you.'

'You didn't tell me,' he reminded her drily. 'Why is it so important for you to prove you can cope alone? That you don't need anyone?'

Becca's eyes narrowed. 'No, I just don't need *you*.'

Her childish retort emerged sounding mean and spiteful. She gave a groan and buried her face in her hands.

A couple of minutes later she blotted the dampness on her cheeks with the back of her hand and lifted her head. 'I didn't mean that the way it sounded.'

'Then you do need me?'

'No—yes.' Suddenly too weary to think straight, let alone fight, she sighed. 'I don't know what I mean,' she admitted, scrubbing her eyes like a tired child.

'I think it is probably better if we tell your parents together anyway.'

Becca stared at him and laughed. 'Have you heard a word I've said?'

'I have been listening, but now I think perhaps it is your turn. Do you really expect me to permit you to bring up my child alone?' The brutal truth was hard to deliver to someone who was staring back at him with red-rimmed eyes, but it needed to be said.

Becca closed her eyes and shook her head. She was literally shaking with the force of her feelings. '*Permit?* You will not *permit* me?'

Her shrill interruption did not affect his icily calm delivery. 'Not alone.'

'I don't have a boyfriend.'

'A situation that is hardly likely to last for ever,' he contended.

Becca, her lips set in an angry straight line, folded her arms across her chest. 'Not your business,' she gritted, thinking that Christos was going to be an impossible act for any man to follow.

He bared his teeth in a white, angry smile and ripped at the collar of his shirt, revealing a small section of olive-brown skin. Becca's stomach gave a lazy flip. She closed her eyes, cursing her weakness, and for an indulgent moment imagined the touch of her lips on his heated skin.

'If you were a free, single agent I'd agree with you. But you're not. You are carrying a child. My child. I will not have my child brought up by another man, Becca.'

'I wouldn't do that!' She felt physically nauseated to discover just how low his opinion of her was.

'I intend to make sure that you don't. You are obviously a very impulsive woman.'

Pretty hard to dispute that, she thought. Eyes narrowed into tearful blue slits, she focused on his lean face. 'I will always put my baby first.'

'Then marry me, and your baby will have everything he needs—including a father.'

'It's not that simple.'

'Oh, but it is that simple. Simple, and not negotiable. You marry me, or I will contest your custody of this child.'

She went cold all over and sucked in a shaky breath. 'You're not serious,' she said, even though she could see he was. If there could ever be a physical representation of *implacable* his expression was it.

'I would suggest you do not try and test that theory.' The dark line along the crest of his sculpted cheekbones suggested he was close to losing his grip on his volatile Greek temper.

'Don't threaten me, Christos.'

Under his tan Christos was as pale as Becca was. 'You act as though marrying me would be a fate worse than death.'

'No court would give you custody.'

'It is true that the legal system favours the mother, but could you take the risk?' He watched the remaining colour drain from her cheeks and tried not to feel like a total bastard.

'If you blackmail me I'll be the wife of your nightmares.'

He sketched a grin. 'I'll take that as a yes, shall I?'

'One of these days you won't get your own way, and I hope I'll be there to see it.'

Had she been in the mood to notice such things, Becca would have seen that he looked tired and relieved rather than triumphal.

'That's all you've got to show for an entire morning's shopping?' Erica teased when she met her for lunch.

'They're nice shoes,' Becca said defensively as she replaced her purchases in the bag. The price label had seemed obscene to her, but she had succumbed when she saw how long and elegant they made her legs look.

Becca ordered fish and a salad. When the waiter had gone she noticed the price of her scallops and gasped. 'That's so expensive! I should have ordered the chicken,' she fretted.

'You're about to marry one of the richest men in Europe—if not the world, for that matter—and you're worried about not ordering the cheapest thing on the menu! As for the shoes,' Erica added, looking at the package on the empty seat. 'The man has given you an empty chequebook and you buy one pair of shoes and worry about it. You really are hopeless, Becca,' she said, looking amused.

'I don't need anything else,' Becca retorted weakly. 'Except for a dress for the wedding, and I didn't really see anything I—'

'Could afford?' Erica teased. 'I can see you need a few lessons in shopping. After lunch,' she promised. 'Now, what about some wine?' Becca looked alarmed and Erica grinned. 'Don't worry, in deference to your stress levels I'll join you and have a glass of mineral water. But you're really going to have to get used to the fact that you don't have to balance the books at the end of the month any more. You're going to be the disgustingly rich Mrs Carides. You're not paying.'

But I am, Becca thought dully. I'm paying with my freedom. So much had been crammed into the past three weeks that she had not had much time to think about the step she was taking.

At the end of the day, despite the fact that she'd successfully resisted her sister's blandishments over several purchases, there still seemed to be an awful lot of clothes lying on the hotel bed—including a genuine vintage thirties dress she had seen and fallen in love with. Sleeveless, with a scooped neckline, the heavily beaded cream silk creation reached mid-calf.

'What do you think?' she had asked Erica as she'd emerged from the changing room.

Erica had shrugged, and by way of reply had looked at the price label. 'You'll look great. But I think you could do better,' she'd said, shaking her head. 'You're marrying a billionaire. You do realise that all you have to do is pick up the phone and designers will be fighting to dress you?'

'I've been dressing myself for twenty-six years and I think I'll continue, if you don't mind.'

'You know what I mean.'

'I do. If you've got it—or in this case if Christos has got it—you should flaunt it.'

'Well, isn't it tempting?'

'No.'

Erica gave her sister a quick, affectionate hug. 'You really are the world's worst conspicuous consumer, aren't you?'

'Perhaps you should marry him yourself?' Becca suggested tartly.

Erica watched as her sister tried to see her rear view in the mirror. 'Don't think I wouldn't cut you out if I had half a chance,' she teased.

'Feel free.'

Becca's tone brought her sister's frowning regard to her face. 'You do know I'm joking, right?'

'Of course I do.'

Erica's concerned frown evaporated and she gave an impish grin. 'Well, even if I did want to steal him off you I wouldn't stand a chance. You know, the other evening I had been telling him about my nursing course, talking for ten minutes at least, when he looked at me and said, "Did you say something?" And,' she recounted, her mock indignation escalating as she recalled the unbelievable slight, 'On Tuesday he forgot my name! He called me Emma!' The recollection made her eyes dance with laughter.

'Christos has a lot on his mind at the moment,' Becca said. 'Maybe he's one of those people who just aren't good with names.'

'You won't be sticking up for him if he forgets *your* name,' Erica predicted with a grin. 'Not that that's likely.'

'You don't think so?' asked Becca absently as she gathered the heavy beaded skirt in one hand and prepared to go back into the changing room.

'Heavens no. He hardly takes his eyes off you. You must have noticed,' she added, giving her head an incredulous little shake when Becca looked at her with blank astonishment. 'He's clearly got a thing about redheads.' Erica could not keep a hint of wistful envy from her voice as she added ruefully, 'Or at least about you.'

There was a moment of startled silence before Becca smiled at her sister. The sparkle in her eyes faded and she said, in a voice that didn't even hint at the depth of her churning emotions, 'Aren't I the lucky one?'

It only lasted for a moment, but for that instant Becca knew what it would feel like if Christos returned her feelings.

Almost immediately common sense reasserted itself and presented an entirely more plausible explanation for Christos's constant scrutiny.

Of course the man watched her—within hours of installing her in the luxurious hotel suite she presently occupied he must have realised that he had lumbered himself with a woman who was social liability.

The man is watching you like a hawk because he's afraid you'll use the wrong fork, or offend someone important!

But she would never forget that moment when she had allowed herself to hope.

'You know,' Erica confided, her teasing expression fading as she smoothed back her long blonde hair from her face, 'I sort of feel responsible for you and Christos getting together—writing to him and everything. I mean he could have been a total bastard, like Alex, and then I'd have felt terrible.'

'But you've decided he's not, have you?'

Erica laughed. 'Are you kidding? Behind the bossiness and that dark, brooding exterior he's one of the good guys—and anyway, he's crazy about you.'

And she believed it, Becca realised. Maybe, she reflected, the younger girl was seeing what she wanted to. Not trusting herself to respond, Becca gave a quick smile and, twitching the curtain, stepped inside the changing booth.

Despite the lukewarm reception to her dress Becca had remained firm, and now, as she tried it on again, she was glad she had. She was pirouetting in front of the full-length mirror when there was a knock on the bedroom door.

A quick glance at her watch told her it was thirty minutes after the time she'd arranged to meet Christos, her parents and her future mother-in-law in the restaurant. She cursed softly under her breath.

'Hold on a minute!' she yelled.

It was several minutes later when she appeared at the door, her cheeks pink from the exertion of fighting her way out of the dress, with a hotel robe belted tightly around her middle.

Seeing Christos standing there, looking predictably gorgeous, robbed her of the ability to speak. So Becca simply stared at him, feeling a confusing mixture of antagonism and lustful longing until, looking extremely impatient, he broke the silence.

'There is a problem?' You didn't have to be particularly intuitive to notice that he was in a vile mood.

'Why would there be a problem?' she countered warily.

'You were to meet our respective parents with me.' His dark brows drew into a straight line as he consulted his watch. 'Forty-five minutes ago.'

'Thirty-five,' she couldn't help correcting.

A nerve clenched along his jaw as his glance slid to her mouth. 'I stand corrected.'

'No...' She drew a sigh and he looked expectant, in the slightly bored, supercilious way that was unique to him. With anyone else she would have been the first to cheerfully apologise if she was late, so why was apologising to him like pulling teeth?

'I lost track of time and, no, before you say anything,' she warned, 'I *didn't* forget on purpose. I was trying on my wedding dress.'

His eyes swept downwards and Becca was suddenly very conscious that she was naked beneath her robe. She clutched the lapels together at the neck.

'And is it a nice dress?'

As if he was interested. His observant eyes caught her sliding her hand down the neckline of her dressing gown, to ease the chafing of the heavy fabric against her sensitised nipples, and she snatched it away, blushing.

'It makes me look less fat than the others did.' She was almost looking forward to the stage when she was obviously pregnant, because right now she just looked—and felt—fat and shapeless.

'You're not *fat!*' Luscious and ripe were the adjectives that came to Christos as he looked at her.

His astonishment appeared genuine, which made Becca's attitude towards him thaw fractionally as she advised gruffly, 'I'd reserve judgement until you've seen me in it, if I were you.'

'I will—in a few days' time.'

The reminder sent a flash of pure panic through her body. Was it really only days away?

Calm. Be calm, she told herself sternly. *Don't think about it!*

'Let me see you in this dress now, and I'll give my informed opinion.'

Soon I'll have to think about it. Soon it will be a reality.

'You want to see me in my wedding dress?' She shook her head and made an effort to focus. 'Oh, no. It's unlucky for the groom to see it before the day,' she reminded him.

'You are superstitious?'

'Not especially, but let's face it—we need all the luck we can get.'

His dark gaze swept up from her bare toes.

She read the anger in his deepset eyes. 'It's the truth,' she insisted defiantly. 'The truth shouldn't annoy you. Though,' she added as a muttered addition, 'just about everything else I do or say does.' Which did not exactly bode well for a life of togetherness, she thought dully.

'By all means let's embrace the truth,' he retorted, flashing the sort of smile that she was learning to mistrust. 'And in that same spirit of openness and honesty, may I ask you something?'

'I suppose so,' she agreed cautiously.

Christos heard himself ask the question that had been uppermost in his mind since she had opened the door. 'Are you wearing any clothes underneath that thing?'

CHAPTER ELEVEN

OVERPOWERINGLY aware of the heat explosion in the vulnerable core of her body, she slung a hard, angry smile in his direction. 'Very funny.'

'I was not trying to be funny. I actually don't find it at all funny that I can think of very little else but having you in my bed.'

He found himself thinking about this subject at the most inappropriate moments—like during his meeting earlier that day. When he had realised that he had no recollection at all of the previous half-hour's delicate negotiations, he had had to excuse himself, much to the astonishment of the others present.

Ironically later, his second-in-command had been full of awe and admiration, assuming it had been part of some fiendishly clever strategy on his part.

This blurring of his personal and work life was something he had never before experienced—he had *never* struggled to compartmentalise his life.

'You look shocked,' he said, examining the pale contours of her delicately moulded face. 'It's hardly news that I am attracted to you, is it?'

His dark lashes swept downwards and his restless glance moved to the blue-veined pulse-spot that beat frantically at the base of her throat.

'Or that you are attracted to me.' Under his steady gaze she went bright red, a response he seemed to take as confirmation of his assertion. 'Which makes your bizarre insistence on pre-wedding night abstinence all the more baffling.'

'But you said…'

There will be no need to bolt your door. I may be prepared to blackmail you into marriage, but my bed you will come to willingly, yineka mou.

That had been what he'd said. She had played it back in her head often enough to be word-perfect.

On that occasion Becca had fired back a derisive, 'Don't hold your breath! No—on second thoughts do.' And he had laughed in a way that suggested he didn't think for a second she'd hold out.

Maybe he was right.

The trouble stemmed from the fact that she had lost control. Since she had agreed to the wedding he had been laying down the law and she had been meekly complying. At least that was the way it felt. Although she was genuinely worried about how he would react to her rapidly changing body, her ill-thought-out insistence that he wasn't going to be sharing her bed until after the wedding had been mostly an attempt to take back some control.

Of course she had shot herself in the foot—because she had been dying of frustration ever since that first night, when he had installed her in the luxury hotel suite and left without even touching her!

'I didn't think you were bothered.' She heard the resentment in her voice and bit her lip.

'Then you are wrong. I am. Very.' His lips formed a twisted grin as he used the word. 'I am so *bothered*,' he revealed from between gritted teeth, 'that I can barely function.'

Thank heavens it's not just me!

The relief she felt at not having voiced her thought out loud faded as she encountered the glitter of hot, raw desire in his gaze. She gave a ragged gasp as all the muscles low in her belly tightened.

She tried to respond with a scornful smile. But her face

felt stiff and her voice, when she spoke, was strained and shaky.

'The next thing you'll be telling me is you're marrying me because I'm so irresistible.'

Anger and frustration flashed in his dark eyes.

This was the first time he had given a hint that it concerned him one way or the other. 'Can you forget the damned marriage for one second?'

Having spent an hour that afternoon with his mother, who had talked about nothing else, he found it was not his favourite subject. He wished he had just dragged Becca off to the nearest register office

Hands set on her slim hips, breathing hard, Becca followed him inside her hotel suite. 'I'd love to forget it!' she yelled at his back.

After moving restlessly around the sitting room of her suite Christos picked up an apple from the laden fruit bowl and put it down again, his expression sour as he muttered something under his breath.

Becca felt sick. Of course he resented the fact he was being forced into marriage because of his old-fashioned belief that there was no other way to raise a child. She had no idea why she felt so hurt and shocked. Any man in his situation would feel the same.

'Don't you think I've *tried* to forget it?' she challenged. 'But it's pretty damned hard when you've got this damned rock on your finger!' she yelled, pointing at the square-cut sapphire surrounded by diamonds that he had casually produced and announced she should wear.

'You don't like the ring—fine,' he said, dismissing it with a casual shrug. 'I will get you another. When I saw it I thought that it matched your eyes.'

An expression of astonishment washed across her features. 'You chose it?' she said, shaking her head in a confused negative motion.

His brows lifted. 'Who did you think chose it?'

'I assumed you'd got one of your minions to buy it.' As someone who found it terribly hard to ask anyone to do anything, and therefore usually ended up doing it herself Becca envied his ability to delegate.

Before Christos could respond the phone in his pocket began to shrill. She stood there while he listened and then spoke into it in his own language.

'My mother,' he explained, sliding it back into his pocket. 'She and your parents were concerned that you had been taken ill when you didn't turn up as arranged. Your parents said you're never late.'

'And you weren't concerned, I suppose?' She whisked around, and found herself looking directly into the large mirror that was set on the wall.

To her dismay Christos came to stand behind her, and their reflected eyes meshed in the mirror. 'I have learnt over the past days that you are more robust than you appear,' he observed, looking at her slender ramrod-stiff back.

She swung back. 'You mean I won't agree with every decision you make?' she suggested sweetly.

'This campaign you have to retain your independence is quite unnecessary, you know,' he told her mildly.

'I don't know what you mean.'

His lips twisted into an ironic smile as their eyes locked. 'I have no taste for docile women, *agape mou*.'

Becca's heart began to thud heavy and slow in her chest as he carried on looking at her. Her eyelids felt hot as she stared back. The enervating wave of lustful longing that threatened to submerge her made it an effort not to fall over, and her knees felt strangely disconnected from the rest of her body.

Do you have a taste for me?

Before the compulsion to voice her unspoken question became too strong to resist she took a deep, restorative breath and picked up her bag from the table, pretending to search for something inside.

'Please don't run away with the idea that I care one way or the other what sort of woman does it for you.' Closing her bag, she gave an amused laugh.

His hooded eyes fixed on the back of her burnished head, he took a step towards her.

'I think you already know.'

Becca felt her control slip another fatal notch and took another deep breath before turning around. 'You really don't need to flirt with me just because we're getting married.'

'Who would you suggest I flirt with?'

'I don't care,' she snapped.

He ran a finger down her cheek. 'Liar,' he taunted, and felt her shiver.

Breathing hard, Becca turned her head away. 'Is it a total disaster?'

'What are we talking here? My lack of success in seducing my future wife?'

Well aware that her own irritability had a lot to do with frustration, Becca snapped back tetchily, 'Don't be stupid. We both know that you could seduce an iceberg with your eyes closed if you wanted to.'

Eyes gleaming with laughter, he admitted, 'I much prefer to keep my eyes open. I like to watch your face,' he confided in a raw, sexy voice that stripped her nerve-endings bare.

'I was talking about my parents and your mother,' she explained hoarsely. If ever there was a mismatch it was the glamorous widow of a Greek tycoon and her own very ordinary parents.

His eyes narrowed. 'Why would you assume it's a disaster?'

'You're not serious? Well, my parents and your mother

are hardly going to have a lot in common, are they?' she pointed out, clasping her hands together to hide the fact they were still visibly shaking as she pretended to study herself in the mirror.

'They have their future grandchild in common. And even if they didn't, they appear to be getting on very well.'

'Well, don't expect me to pretend to be something I'm not just to impress your mother,' she warned him darkly.

A bewildered expression on his face, Christos touched her shoulder and gently pulled her around until she was facing him. 'Why would I want you to be anyone but yourself?'

As if *herself* was someone who would marry a Carides!

Becca stated the obvious. 'Well, I'm hardly the sort of girl your average Greek tycoon marries, am I?' She bit down on her lower lip, disgusted by the self-pitying quiver that had entered her voice.

'You are very fond of labels, aren't you, Becca?'

The accusation made her blink. 'No, of course I'm not.'

His hands slid down her shoulders. Twisting his fingers into hers, he brought her hands up to his lips. Becca's insides melted.

'You have no need to be insecure. You will be my wife. My wife does not need anyone's approval.'

Your wife needs love, though. *Your* love, Becca thought to herself.

Adopting a businesslike attitude that gave no hint of her desperate yearning, she lifted her head and smiled.

'Will you please tell our parents that I'll be along directly?'

His lips formed a twisted smile as he saw her glance flicker significantly towards the door. 'No problem,' he said, releasing her hands. 'I will wait.'

She slung him a frustrated glare. 'Then it will take longer,' she warned him.

His broad shoulders lifted. 'How so?'

She looked at her toes. 'You make me nervous.' She lifted her head and caught a dangerously speculative expression on his face. His dark eyes brushed hers and she fled.

Inside the relative safety of the bathroom, she leaned against the door and, her eyes closed, sighed.

Two days! She seriously doubted she would last!

As she walked through the lobby with Christos at her side she was uncomfortably aware of the way people turned and stared. She was under no illusion as to who they were staring at. She looked up curiously, to see if Christos was irritated, and discovered that he appeared totally oblivious to the fact that he was the centre of attention.

When a woman about to enter a lift saw them and stopped, unashamedly staring, it was the final straw for Becca, who hissed, 'Is it always like this?' A future of being gawped at, her appearance being analysed and criticised by total strangers, because of who she was married to filled her with horror.

He slowed and looked down at her. 'Is *what* always like this?'

'Do people stare at you wherever you go?'

Before he had an opportunity to respond the hotel manager, an incredibly elegant silver-haired man, who wore extremely smart suits and had an air of calm efficiency, appeared at their side.

The manager nodded respectfully to Becca and expressed the hope that she was enjoying her stay. Clearly the fact that Christos was picking up the bill gave her VIP status in this man's eyes.

She assured him everything was marvellous, which it was, and the man turned his attention to Christos.

'Your secretary has left a message at Reception, sir,' he said.

Christos looked surprised. 'She has?'

'Apparently she wasn't able to contact you on your mobile.'

'Which is why I turned it off,' Christos observed, looking irritated. 'I should see what she wants,' he admitted. 'You go ahead, Becca, and I'll catch up. This shouldn't take a moment.'

Becca just stood there. 'No, I'll wait for you.'

Already turning, he slid her a quick impatient look, failing to identify the note of panic in her voice. 'They are waiting for you—go ahead.'

Her jaw tightened. She knew they were waiting for her—that was the problem! His mother would hate her on sight, of that she had totally convinced herself, and she was furious with herself for caring about this unknown woman's approval. Despite Christos's assertion that he didn't give a damn what anyone else thought, she felt sure his mother's disapproval, even if it was polite, would mean something.

Even if the protection his presence at her side offered was mostly in her mind, as she watched him vanish from her view Becca decided that a man with an ounce of sensitivity would have realised she was scared stiff and offered a bit of support!

Do you really think he's going to be there to hold your hand in awkward moments? Get used to it, Becca, she told herself sternly. *Being a babysitter for an insecure wife is going to be way down his list of priorities. In fact* you *are going to be way down his list of priorities.*

She was so lost in her angry, resentful thoughts that a man had virtually thrust his face into hers before she even noticed he was there. Becca instinctively recoiled at the sudden intrusion, and blinked.

The first explanation that offered itself to her was that the stranger was drunk. 'Excuse me,' she said pleasantly.

'Becca, isn't it?'

She looked at him blankly, wondering if she was meant to know who he was. 'Sorry—I don't think I know—?' She broke off as somewhere to her right a blinding flash went off. It was followed in quick succession by several more. Disorientated, she blinked.

'So when's the wedding, love?' the man asked, in the same chummy manner.

The shock of realising she had been waylaid by a reporter held her immobile for a moment.

'Let's have a shot of the ring, Becca.'

Becca automatically put her hand behind her back and looked around frantically. But there was no sign of Christos.

'Excuse me,' she said, adopting a nervous, frigid expression as she attempted to step past him. The man moved, effectively blocking her access to the dining room.

Becca, her temper aroused, was too angry now to be frightened when another flash went off in her face.

'Known him a long time, love? Why are you marrying him, Red?'

'Mind your own business!' she gritted.

He grinned and sneered, 'You marrying him for the money, Red?'

'No, I'm marrying him because he's very good in bed,' she snapped. 'In fact he's the best sex I've ever had!'

The guy's mouth fell open in shock, before an appreciative gleam of delight appeared in his eyes. He had no opportunity to respond, however, because the next second Christos was there, looking tall and menacing. With his face like thunder he hauled the man away from her with such force he almost jerked him off his feet.

'Not the suit, mate!' the younger man cried jokingly. Then he saw Christos's face and his smirk faded.

'Christos, don't!' Becca reached out urgently and caught his arm. 'For heaven's sake, he'd love you to take a pop at him. He'd be able to sell the story for loads!'

'Listen to the lady!' the reporter croaked.

Becca was thinking that if Christos did listen it would be a first when to her intense relief the cavalry, in the shape of hotel security, arrived on the scene. They were large, well-spoken individuals, wearing nice suits and no-nonsense expressions.

Their fortuitous arrival would, she reflected darkly, have been even more fortuitous if they had got there before she'd opened her big mouth.

There was no unseemly tussle. The reporter did not resist as he was firmly but discreetly frogmarched out of Reception.

Christos, standing with his bunched fists clenched at his sides, spat an epithet in his own tongue as he watched the reporter being expelled. Apparently sensing her eyes on his face, he looked down, making an obvious effort to control his feelings as he raked a hand through his dark hair.

'That was intolerable.'

Becca's eyes widened as he framed one side of her face with a big hand. The breath caught in her throat as his strong thumb stroked the curve of her cheek. The unexpected tenderness in his action made her eyes fill.

'You are okay?' Feeling her quiver, he frowned. 'Those people are scum.'

'I'm fine,' she said, wondering how furious he was going to be, on scale of one to ten, when he found out what she had said. *Why did I say that?* 'The man has to make a living, I suppose.' *And I just paid for his summer holiday. And maybe Christmas too.*

'From invading people's privacy and publishing lies?'

An image of the next day's tabloid headlines flashed before her eyes and she felt sick. She had already discovered that Christos guarded his privacy zealously, and that any friend of his who spoke out of turn to the press about him would no longer be considered a friend.

'I am *so* sorry that happened.' She could hear the self-reproach in his deep voice as he added, 'I am to blame. I shouldn't have left you alone.'

The slick manager appeared, looking uncharacteristically ruffled. He was extremely contrite as he drew them to the privacy of an alcove, where they were screened by a lush arrangement of plants from the prying eyes of others. 'Our guests' privacy and security is paramount to us. I assure you that this sort of thing does not happen in our hotel.'

'It did.'

The inescapable truth of Christos's blunt, unsmiling retort brought an uncomfortable flush to the older man's face. He nodded. 'And for that we are very sorry.' He turned to Becca. 'I hope the unfortunate incident has not made you think too badly of us, Miss…?'

Becca, very conscious of Christos's protective arm now encircling her waist—or what passed for her waist these days—smiled and lied with credible calm.

'No harm done.' If only that were true, she thought, dropping her chin to avoid the searching sweep of Christos's dark eyes. She was convinced that her guilt had to be written in neon letters across her forehead.

The men exchanged a few more words, but Becca didn't really pay much attention to what they were saying. She was thinking about how she was going to come clean and admit what she had said to the reporter. Considering Christos was guaranteed to go ballistic when he found out what she had said, it probably ought to be done in a public place.

After the manager had left Christos motioned her to sit down. 'Can I get you something to drink? Tea?'

She shook her head. 'No—I'm fine, thank you.'

'Do you really feel up to this meal?'

'What part of *I'm fine* didn't you understand?' she snapped, leaping to her feet.

For a moment Christos watched, the expression in his dark hooded eyes inscrutable as she paced back and forth, rubbing her hands up and down her forearms. A nerve clenched in his cheek and he muttered forcefully, 'Stop!'

Startled, Becca did as he said. She was expecting to see annoyance on his face, but the tenderness in his expression took her breath away. She didn't resist as he took her hands, which were clasped tight around her own forearms, and laid them flat against his chest. Her wide eyes locked with his and a shiver rippled through her body.

'It's an understandable reaction.' She stiffened, then relaxed slightly as he added, 'You've had a nasty experience.'

'It was a bit of a shock,' she admitted. 'What I don't understand is how he knew who I was—or about our marriage?'

Christos's eyes narrowed. 'I think I do,' he said grimly, and then, without explaining what he meant, he bent his dark head towards her. 'You're coping very well with this, you know.'

Becca almost groaned. His admiration only made her feel even more wretchedly guilty. 'Actually, I'm falling apart—and we both know it.'

Fortunately Christos didn't know the real reason for that. He didn't have the faintest idea what his closeness was doing to her. How feeling the heat of his hard male body through the layers of clothes that separated them made her dissolve inside.

Becca's eyes closed as if she could feel the slow, heavy

thud of his heartbeat under her fingers. He covered them with his own hands, making it impossible for her to remove them even had she wanted to. Which, needless to say, she didn't.

CHAPTER TWELVE

'THESE people can get under your skin,' he admitted. 'Especially when you're not accustomed to the intrusion.'

'And you are?'

He nodded in response to her tentative suggestion. 'I am,' he agreed. 'I should have warned you this was likely to happen at some point. The best thing with paparazzi,' he explained, 'is not to say anything at all.'

Oh, no! 'Right.'

'Just don't react.'

'I'll remember,' she promised gravely, resisting the temptation to ask if strangling a member of the press could be termed *not reacting*.

'It doesn't actually matter what you say.' *That's all you know,* she thought. 'They will always twist it.'

'In fact,' she observed brightly, 'you might read something that you didn't say at all. At least not intentionally.'

'What did you say to him, Becca?'

She had to tell him some time, and now was as good a time as any. She opened her mouth, but as he looked at her expectantly she wimped out and shook her head.

'You know, I really don't recall. Don't you think we should go in to dinner? The parents will wonder what's happened.'

'Suddenly you're very eager.'

'I'm hungry,' she lied.

Having said goodnight to their respective parents, Christos insisted on escorting her back to her room. They reached her bedroom door.

Christos released her arm and tilted his head towards her. His attitude was that of a stranger as he said, 'Goodnight.' Before turning to leave her.

Becca turned her key in the lock, then gave a sigh and spun around. Christos was already some way down the long hotel corridor. 'No!' she called out after him 'Don't go, Christos!'

After the slightest pause in his step he carried on walking. Assuming he hadn't heard her, Becca was about to run after him when he stopped and turned.

Becca's throat dried as he stood there, his head a little to one side in a questioning attitude. Frustrated by her inability to read his expression from this distance, she took a hesitant step forward.

'You want something?'

As Becca opened her mouth the door beside him opened, and she waited until the bearded young man who'd stepped out had reached the lift before nodding.

'Yes, I want you. That is...' she corrected, relieved now that she *couldn't* see his expression '...not *want*, exactly. I—'

'That is a blow to my male ego.'

'This is no joke, Christos,' she reproached him. 'There's something I have to tell you. You're not going to like it,' she warned him, going inside her room and switching on the light.

When he came in she had already taken up a seat on the sofa. 'I hope you don't mind if I take these off. They're agony.' She could feel his eyes on her and sense his impatience as she slid off her high heels.

As a delaying tactic it didn't offer much respite.

Christos stood waiting while she tucked her feet under her.

The pause before he broke the lengthening silence had little to do with his patience and understanding, and quite a lot to do with the fact that her action had caused her skirt to ride up, revealing the lacy tops of her hold-up stockings and a section of bare flesh!

'So, what am I not going to like?' he asked, thinking about how silky her skin had felt under his hands.

Reluctance etched in every line of her face, Becca stopped avoiding looking at him and saw he seemed unusually preoccupied.

'Your mother was very nice to me.'

Her blatant procrastination caused his lips to quiver with amusement. 'They do say confession is good for the soul.' Loosening his tie, he lowered his lean frame onto the sofa beside her.

Becca, noting that he looked mellow and relaxed, felt irrationally resentful. 'Not always good for shaky relationships.'

Her tight-lipped retort caused his brows to lift as he suggested. 'So you think couples should have secrets?'

She shook her head impatiently. 'No, of course I don't. That isn't what I'm saying at all,' she retorted, missing the gleam of sardonic humour in his eyes.

'Oh? I thought for a second there you were an advocate of the ''What they don't know won't hurt them'' school of thought?' he murmured innocently.

'If you are you asking if I'll turn a blind eye if you fool around the answer is no. And,' she added darkly, 'I don't give a damn how discreet you are!' She paused for breath and continued in a more moderate tone, 'I probably should have mentioned this before,' she admitted.

'That you expect fidelity from your husband? Most people would not call that an unreasonable request. I'd go so far as to suggest that most would say you should be able to take that for granted.'

'Yes, if it were a normal marriage I expect they would. But ours will be a marriage of convenience. I suppose you thought I might not mind too much if you carried on much as before.'

'And how would that be?'

Her reproachful blue eyes met his teasing stare head-on. 'I don't have the faintest idea about the lifestyle of a playboy billionaire,' she admitted. 'But I'm assuming it involves doing pretty much what you want, when you want, and,' she added with a swallow, 'with who you want.'

'A billionaire would not stay that way very long if he lived the debauched life of unrestrained hedonism you appear to be visualising, *yineka mou*. I have been known to put in the odd fourteen-hour working day,' he observed drily, 'which actually leaves little time for carousing.'

'I know you work.' Having already observed at first hand his work ethic, she felt qualified to comment on his ability to operate when most people would have succumbed to exhaustion. 'But you're hardly a monk, are you?'

'No, I am not a monk. But what I did before we were engaged to be married does not concern you.'

This gentle remonstrance brought a militant sparkle to Becca's eyes. 'No, but what you do after we're married does.'

It wasn't as if there would be a shortage of women willing to compensate Christos for his loveless marriage. And no doubt some would dream of taking her place one day.

'Yes.'

Becca blinked and regarded him suspiciously. 'What do you mean? You agree?' She was unable to hide her astonishment.

'Certainly I agree.' He gave a shrug. 'This surprises you?'

She studied him, trying to gauge his sincerity. 'Yes, it does,' she admitted gruffly.

'You wish our marriage to be more than cosmetic? That is what you're saying?'

Am I? 'I suppose I am,' she admitted uncertainly.

'Then we are of one mind in this.'

Robbed of an argument, she had little choice but to come clean.

'Should I take this personally?' he asked, when she scooted without thinking to the other side of the sofa.

'Sorry.' She grimaced, flashing him an absent half-smile. 'I can't think when you're near me, and this is hard enough as it is.'

Unaware that she had said anything to produce the flicker of hot emotion in his eyes, she tapped her lip with her forefinger.

'I really don't know why I did it...' she faltered.

'Did what, *yineka mou*?'

Becca lifted her eyes to his and shook her head. 'Please don't be nice to me. It makes me feel even more wretched. I won't blame you for being furious.'

'I will do my best to oblige you, and be suitably furious—but don't you think you should tell me what I'm supposed to be furious about first?'

'This is so difficult—and embarrassing,' she muttered under her breath.

'I'm still living in the hope that you will tell me what you have done before I go totally grey,' he said, sounding weary.

'When you asked me about that reporter I lied.' Her eyes slid guiltily from his. Eyes closed, she took a deep breath and hunched her shoulders. 'I did say something to him...something I probably shouldn't have. No—cancel that. I *definitely* shouldn't have. I've no idea why I said it. I was angry, and he was so revolting, and it just came out.'

'What did you say?'

Her chin lifted. 'Word for word?'

'A close approximation will do.'

'He asked me why I was marrying you.'

A look of understanding spread across his face. 'So you told him about the baby? Not the way I would have chosen to announce it, but it is nothing for you to lose sleep over.'

She shook her head. 'No, I didn't tell him about the baby.'

Christos heaved a deep sigh and clamped his hand to his forehead. '*Becca—!*'

Once she started talking the words tripped over one another. 'All right. I might have said something like you're very good in bed and suggested that you're the best sex I've ever had. Which really isn't as much of a recommendation as it might sound, because frankly there isn't much competition. I know it was crude and vulgar, but I swear I didn't mean to say it. It just came out.'

The stunned silence stretched until her shredded nerve-endings began to scream.

'Thirty seconds. You were talking to him for thirty seconds, tops. I tremble to think what you'd have disclosed to the world's press if I hadn't come along when I did.'

Her startled eyes flew to his face. Her jaw dropped. She had been eaten up with remorse, beating herself up all through that interminable dinner, and he was *laughing*!

She drew herself up and dealt him a killer glare. 'You think this is *funny*?'

He shot out a hand and cupped the back of her head, sinking his fingers into the thickness of her silky curls as he splayed his long fingers to cradled her skull.

'I think you are delightful.'

His incredible eyes stayed on her face while his husky voice made her skin tingle.

She had never heard that the scalp contained any erogenous zones, but his fingers seemed to have located some anyhow. Tomorrow she might look it up...but right now she thought she might just enjoy it.

'You're not angry?'

'It was unfortunate.'

'Aren't you afraid that you'll have a wife who blabs every time someone sticks a camera in her face?'

'I'm much more concerned about having a wife who doesn't want me in her bed.'

'It's not that I don't *want* you in my bed. It's just that I'm quite big...' The books she had read all suggested that she should barely be showing at four months, whereas her bump was far from discreet. 'Clothes hide a multitude of sins, and the truth is not all men are turned on by pregnant women.'

'*That* is the reason you have put me through weeks of torture and more cold showers than can be good for any man?' He took hold of her chin and dragged her face up to his. 'I find you beautiful and desirable, and quite frankly it offends me to hear you denigrate yourself that way.'

'You haven't seen me naked recently,' she retorted.

'That can be remedied now,' he added, drawing her to her feet and looking at her in a way that made her insides dissolve.

'Christos...'

He effectively stilled her protest with his lips and led her through to the bedroom. The way he managed to strip off her clothes while not breaking eye contact for one second spoke of the sort of experience she didn't let herself think about.

She had enough body image issues as it was!

Christos, to her intense relief, did not. He was fascinated by the new heaviness and sensitivity of her breasts, and the gentle mound of her belly didn't seem to bother him at all.

Lying next to him in bed, she touched his warm skin and gave a deep sigh of pleasure. 'I'm really glad we're doing this. I've felt so...'

'Cranky?' he suggested with a smile in his voice.

'Well, yes.'

'You're amazing,' he said, propping himself up on his elbows to look down on her voluptuous curves. 'I want to taste every inch of you.'

'It might take a long time.'

'I have all night.'

She gave a slow, sultry smile and ran a hand down the flat of his belly. 'In that case maybe I could taste you?'

His eyes were filled with a feverish brilliance as they locked with hers. 'I'm all yours.'

Becca took him at his word.

It was four in the morning when the taxi drew up outside Christos's London home. Asking the driver to wait, Becca got out. Even though she was not wearing a coat, she barely noticed that the temperature had dropped below zero. She stood for a moment, with her bare fingers closed around a wrought-iron railing that was already silvered with frost, gathering her courage.

The elegant square of tall, imposing early Georgian residences was deserted, and with a heart thudding loudly in trepidation she mounted the shallow flight of steps that led to the intimidatingly large, shiny front door.

She took a deep breath and, feeling strangely disconnected from what she was doing, pressed the intercom button. A disembodied voice responded almost immediately. There was no suggestion of astonishment that she should be calling at this hour, just a polite request for her to state her name and her business.

In a tense voice she responded to the request literally.

'Name…yes, of course,' she said. 'My name is Becca Summer, and I have come to tell Christos that I can't go through with the wedding.'

Unaware that her startlingly literal response had brought about a frenetic flurry of activity within the house, she nod-

ded in response to the slightly delayed assurance that someone would be with her directly.

She nervously wrung her icy hands, unaware that a camera above her head was recording every move she made.

True to the invisible presence's promise, barely a minute
had elapsed when the front door—grand, in keeping with
the rest of the building—was pulled open.

Becca was shocked to see Christos himself standing
there, in bare feet, his dark hair deliciously tousled and with
a defined shadow on his normally cleanshaven jaw. He was
wearing a black robe that ended mid muscular brown
thigh—and, as far as she could see, nothing else whatso-
ever.

The focus she had fought so hard to maintain vanished
in the time it took her to draw a single gulp of cold air into
her lungs. Underneath the fabric she knew his skin would
be warm and smooth to the touch. *Do not go there, Becca!*
The stern command came far too late to halt the stab of
uncontrollable sexual desire that caused the muscles in her
abdomen to clench viciously.

After not breathing at all for the space of several heartbeats, she released a fractured sigh and croaked accusingly,
'You're not asleep.'

'I *was* asleep,' he corrected, dragging both hands through
his dark hair before pressing his fingers to the groove above
his nose. 'And I retain a faint hope that I still am. That any
minute now I will wake up and discover this is all a night-
mare.'

'I'm really sorry to disturb you,' she apologized, thinking, *I'm his bad dream.* 'But I… It couldn't wait. Once I
realised, I had to tell you. The thing is, I can't go through
with this wedding.'

A muscle clenched along his strong, stubble-dusted jaw
as their eyes connected. 'Is that so?'

Becca gave a frustrated frown. Christos didn't seem to

be grasping the seriousness of what she was telling him. 'This isn't a joke. I'm totally serious.'

'So I understand from my housekeeper, who woke me to tell me your news.' The woman—clearly she had drawn the short straw—had taken very good care not to look him in the face as she did so. The memory caused the hard planes and angles of Christos's face to grow taut. 'Do you often discuss our private business with total strangers?'

A flush ran over Becca's fair skin and she grimaced. 'I didn't think,' she admitted.

And from not thinking she had tumbled headlong into thinking the wrong thing. Right now the only thoughts going through her head concerned the fabric belt which had been loosely tied around his waist. The same belt that had now slipped and come to rest on his narrow hips...

What if it slipped a little more? Rather than being shocked by the realisation that she was mentally undressing this man, Becca felt excited.

I'm sexually liberated, she thought, and began to smile— until she saw the way Christos was looking at her. He would definitely consider a giggle inappropriate. Or, worse still, he might ask her what she smiling at. And she might tell him.

That was a very sobering thought!

'Forgive me for not displaying shock, but I have already discovered that not thinking is a way of life for you. It was only three hours ago you kicked me out of your bed.' He was still stinging from that experience. 'I warn you, I don't much like to be treated like a sex toy.'

Becca giggled, and then clamped a hand over her mouth as she caught his murderous glare. 'I wanted to spend the night with you, but I didn't want to see your face when you read the tabloids this morning,' she admitted.

'I don't read the tabloids.'

Gathering the shreds of her shattered will-power, she

dragged her wandering eyes back to his face. 'Let me explain about this—'

'By all means explain,' he said, cutting across her. 'But I do not care to discuss my personal business in the street. And you appear not to be dressed for the weather.'

You have room to talk, she thought, trying not to stare too obviously at the section of hair-dusted golden chest. How could a man sound so stuffy and stern and look so incredibly sexy?

'No, of course not.' She glanced uncomfortably over her shoulder. 'The thing is…the taxi. He's waiting. Shall I tell him to go?'

'Unless you wish to include him with my household in this discussion?'

Becca clenched her teeth and recognised it might have helped her cause if she had been a little less up-front about her reason for calling.

'There is a problem?' he added, scanning her upturned features when she didn't move.

'Sort of,' she admitted, concerned about the fact he could read her so damned well even when she kept her mouth shut. 'The thing is, I think I might have…well, actually, no…I *did* come out without any money, and…'

'You came out without any money?' he repeated, in an astonished voice.

'Not deliberately,' she countered. 'I just need you to pay the man. I'll pay you back,' she heard herself add, ridiculously.

It was no surprise when, after moment's incredulous silence, he threw back his dark head and laughed. 'Just when I thought you could not get more absurd you say something to prove me wrong.'

At least his laughter had taken the edge off the simmering tension between them.

Becca responded to his gesture and entered the house. Inside the warmth of the chandelier-lit hallway, she realised that she was very cold indeed, and shivered.

CHAPTER THIRTEEN

'I WOULD offer you my robe.' Christos touched his lapel. 'But I might be left a little over-exposed.'

Becca felt the heat bloom in her cheeks. He couldn't have known what she was thinking—*could he?*

As he turned to issue an instruction to a uniformed man she studied his profile through the protective shield of her lashes. When the employee had nodded and stepped out of the front door—she presumed to pay the taxi off—Christos's attention shifted immediately back to her. Caught staring like a greedy child in a sweet shop window, she self-consciously lowered her gaze.

Christos reached out and, cupping her chin in his hand, tilted her face up to his. 'You're like ice,' he said with a frown.

'I—'

'I know,' he interceded. 'You didn't think. Do you like the marble?'

'Marble?' she echoed, wondering more how it was possible for the lightest of his touches to be so debilitating than what he was talking about.

'The floor in here—which appears to interest you so much.'

'It's very nice,' she agreed gravely as she tried to still her chattering teeth.

His expression softened. 'Come, we will go into the library. There is a fire lit there.'

She couldn't restrain her curiosity as she followed him. 'How do you know there's a fire?'

'I know because I was in there half an hour ago.'

'You mean you'd only just gone to bed?'

He gave a slight ironic smile in response to her exclamation, and with a hand in the small of her back propelled her ahead of him through a panelled door to the right.

'Do you always work that late?' The glow of embers revealed to Becca's interested gaze a room with wood-panelled walls, bookshelves and a large oak desk on which a laptop was open. There was more proof of recent occupancy, should his word not be proof enough, in the half-full brandy glass on the mantel of the Adam fireplace.

'I was not working.'

'But you said...' She shook her head. 'Sorry, I didn't mean to pry.'

'I could not work.'

Becca puzzled over the undercurrent in his voice as she watched him walk over to the desk. A flick of a switch and the angled reading lamp that sat there lent the masculine room a warm, subdued glow.

Christos closed the laptop with a click. 'My inability to work can hardly surprise you.'

Mutely she shook her head.

He spelt it out. 'I had just been ejected from a warm bed, and I didn't want to sleep alone.'

'Oh,' some demon made her retort spicily, 'I'm sure that could have been solved. All you had to do was pick up the phone...one word and I'm sure there would have been dozens of women eager to hotfoot it over here.' A scowl formed on her face as she brooded on those unknown over-sexed and almost certainly stunningly beautiful women.

A gleam appeared in Christos's dark hooded eyes as he watched her. 'You do know that you sound dangerously like a jealous woman, *yineka mou*?'

Becca, who did know, glared at him. 'For heaven's sake, take that smug look off your face. *Men!*' she muttered, slinging a disdainful look over her shoulder as she walked over to the fire. 'You're all the same.'

Even as she made the disgruntled claim Becca knew that it was totally false. Christos wasn't like any other man. Her Greek lover was utterly and totally unique.

'You think you're totally irresistible.'

'Well, you must take some of the blame for that—telling me there are any number of women willing to leap into my bed if I snap my fingers.'

She had lifted her icy hands to the warmth of the dying flames when a log landed with a thud amongst them, sending up a cloud of sparks.

She turned and found Christos standing very close. She brutally quashed the urge to press her head against his chest. 'You scared me.' But not as much wanting him scared her. 'I suppose you think that all you have to do is snap your fingers and *I'll* be in your bed too?'

'I don't think I will ever take having you in my bed for granted.'

'Because we're only together for the baby?'

'You know that is not the case.'

'The sex, you mean?' *Please say there's more; please say there's more,* she thought, willing him with her eyes to say what she longed to hear. He didn't have to feel the way she did; she could live with less. Less would be more than she had now.

His dark eyes moved over her slim, nervous figure and the silence between them stretched. Finally he gave an odd, twisted smile and said, 'Ah, the sex…what else…?'

Becca silently berated herself for having let herself harbour false hopes. 'You could have that without marriage.'

'You and the baby are a package deal. This light suits you.'

The driven quality to his abrupt addition made her laugh nervously. She lifted a hand to her smooth, unlined face.

'You mean it hides the bags under my eyes and the crow's feet?' Then she recognised the expression of fierce tenderness in his amazing eyes and the laughter locked tight in her throat.

As he covered the space that separated them her anticipation of his touch was so strong she was literally shaking.

'I mean,' he corrected, taking her face between his big hands, 'that it makes you look like you've just stepped out of a Titian. You're a living, breathing work of art.'

Becca's eyes half closed as he tilted her face back. An almost feline sigh of pleasure escaped her parted lips as his mouth, teasingly soft, moved up the entire length of her pale throat. He moved to the corner of her mouth and stopped.

'Your lip is bleeding.'

'It is?' she said vaguely, and lifted a not quite steady hand to her mouth. There was a spot of blood on her finger when she pulled it away. 'I bite my lip when I'm nervous.'

'And I make you feel nervous?'

The sensuous promise in his eyes made her stomach flip lazily.

'I don't know the word for what you make me feel,' she admitted in a throaty whisper.

His head bent closer, close enough for her to feel the tickle of his warm breath as it stirred the fine downy hair on her skin. 'You're still bleeding,' he rasped.

'I am?' she whispered, thinking his eyes were the hottest thing she had ever seen.

'Uhuh…' he grunted, bringing his lithe male body right up against her.

Becca's knees sagged as she felt the hardness of his erection dig into the softness of her belly. She groaned again as she felt the damp brush of his tongue against the fragile broken area on her lips.

'Oh, God!' she moaned in an agonised whisper. 'What are you doing?'

'First aid,' he rasped throatily. 'We should stop the bleeding.'

If he doesn't stop I'll need full-on resuscitation, not first aid, she thought. And if he did stop? What then? Her eyes suddenly snapped open.

'Don't stop!'

The panicky entreaty brought a gleam of male satisfaction to his smoky dark gaze.

'It was not my intention,' he admitted, sliding the soft cashmere cardigan off her shoulders to reveal the bright silk tee shirt she wore beneath. 'You are warm enough?'

Warm? She was on fire! 'I'm fine.'

She quivered as his fingers skimmed over the jewel-bright fabric before sliding underneath to touch the warm skin of her midriff.

'This feels nice,' he told her, fitting his mouth to hers.

After several moments of increasingly frantic kissing she surfaced, gasping for air.

Christos, the sharp angles of his carved cheekbones highlighted by dark bands of colour, allowed his eyes to roam over the soft contours of her face until they stilled on the swollen, full outline of her tremulous lips. '*Very* nice,' he approved throatily.

'It was a gift from your mother.'

She felt the deep rumble of his warm laughter. 'I didn't mean this,' he corrected. And to illustrate his meaning he stroked a fingertip down the length of her spine. When he reached the base he slid his fingers under the waistband of her jeans. 'Your skin is a gift, perhaps,' he conceded. 'But not from my mother.'

Her eyelids felt hot and heavy as she lifted her eyelashes from her cheek, and her senses swam as she focused on his dark face. Her expression was unselfconsciously enthralled when she reached up and trailed a finger down his strong jaw. The sprinkle of dark stubble made her fingertips tingle.

'My God!' she said, her voice thick with emotion. 'You're just so damned perfect that when I look at you I...I just want...' Closing her eyes with an inarticulate shake of her head, she pressed her face against his chest, inhaling the unique scent of his body.

She felt his lips in her hair and it no longer seemed to matter that she was unable to articulate the range and depth of emotions he aroused within her. It was enough just to be here with him.

Why can't life always be this simple?

'Becca...?'

The sound of his thickened voice brought her head up. There was an expression of fascination on his starkly beautiful features as he lifted her hair from her neck and let the burnished strands fall through his fingers.

'*Theos*, but leaving you tonight was hell!'

Her eyes widened. 'I thought you wanted to go.'

'Wanted!' he ejaculated, staring at her as though she was mad. 'Where do you get these weird ideas from? It has occurred to me that we should talk more—then maybe these things would not happen so often?'

'Talking is good. But later, not now,' she pleaded, pushing her fingers deep into his lush dark hair.

She closed her eyes as he claimed her mouth, and felt her insides shift and melt as his tongue made repeated stabbing incursions between her parted lips.

She felt rather than heard him say her name, the sound lost in her mouth as she twisted, straining to press herself closer to him. Imagining her bare skin against his was no longer enough. She reached for the tie on his robe. When the knot would not slip, she let out a frustrated little grunt.

Christos's hand came up to cover her own and she lifted her passion-glazed eyes to his.

'So you have forgotten this nonsense about not going through with the wedding?'

With a sharp cry of horror she pulled away from him.

Christos stood there, looking confused and then angry as she backed away, her hand held to her mouth and her eyes wide and accusing.

'So is that what that was all about? You make love to me and I'll just fall in with whatever you want?' The pain of thinking he could be so calculating made her feel betrayed. She had let down her defences and he had taken advantage. Her lips quivered and she added with a gulp, 'And there was me thinking you *wanted* to make love to me.'

Christos looked at her quivering lip and watched her glorious eyes fill. He swore softly under his breath and gritted in frustration, 'You think I can turn it on and off like a tap?'

Reading the frustration in his angry face, she felt a flicker of uncertainty—which she swiftly repressed. She was in a position to know that when it came to getting what he wanted Christos would have no qualms about using any methods necessary. And he wanted this baby to be a Carides and thought she was threatening to call off the marriage.

'I won't be manipulated!' If only it was that easy! When he touched her she lost her mind—and her will.

'I was not trying to manipulate you,' Christos bit back, very white around the lips as he grabbed his head in both hands and groaned. '*Theos…!*' he yelled, his head lifting. 'I was trying to make love to you. I forget my own name when I make you love to you, but do I accuse you of trying to turn me into an amnesiac?'

'So you didn't think that you could make me change my mind about the wedding by making love to me?' she asked, unable to tear her eyes from the nerve that was ticking away in his lean cheek. *He forgot his own name…?*

'Look, if I wanted to use dirty tactics to coerce you into going through with this wedding I would *not* make love to you.'

Becca, her brow furrowed, watched open-mouthed as he strode back to the fireplace, picked up the half-full glass of amber liquid from the mantel and tossed it back in one gulp.

'I've no idea what you're talking about.'

He slammed the empty glass down and turned back to her. As his dark eyes travelled in a lazy, insolent fashion up and down her body his mouth twisted into a smile that was both cynical and splinteringly sensual.

When he eventually captured her eyes with his dark liquid gaze Becca shivered, and was appalled to recognise the tingle that passed through her body as excitement.

'Let me spell it out for you. You need me.' The cynicism etched in his smile became more deeply ingrained as he added, 'Even if it's only for sex, you need me.'

The heat flew to her cheeks as she finally realised that he thought the threat of *withdrawing* sexual favours could make her do anything he wanted. *And couldn't it?*

'I always knew you were an arrogant piece of work, Christos, but this really... Words fail me...' she revealed, her voice shaking with outrage.

'Not noticeably,' he inserted drily. 'Do you know how I know that you couldn't do without it?' he asked.

The crude question made her compress her lips and stare at him with loathing, while her skin began to burn with humiliated heat.

'Because *I* couldn't. I will return your compliment of earlier: you're the best sex I've ever had too.'

'I told you I wasn't being literal. The reporter just caught me off guard and made me angry and...' Her chest lifted and a deep sigh juddered through her body. 'I am?'

'Yes.' His beautiful lips quivered as he steadily held her gaze.

'And you've had quite a lot of sex,' she murmured thoughtfully. 'In fact probably loads. So that must make me pretty…well, pretty brilliant.' The choking sound that emerged from his lips made her eyes widen. 'Please tell me that I did not say that out loud!' she begged in a mortified whisper.

'It is not a good thing to base a marriage on lies.'

'It's not a good thing to base a marriage on a baby either,' she retorted, wondering if a person could die of mortification.

'And on sexual compatibility,' he reminded her. 'And before you begin a litany of denial—'

'I wasn't going to,' she said, feeling quite absurdly self-conscious as she met his eyes. 'Not being able to look at someone without wanting to rip off that someone's clothes,' she said, looking at the knot on his belt, 'is not a feeling with staying power.' *Or at least I hope not, because I don't think I can take another month of this—let alone years!*

'I am presuming I am that *someone*?'

'I only sleep with one billionaire at a time.'

A flash of annoyance highlighted the subtle shards of gold in Christos's eyes as he gritted, 'I am getting tired of your preoccupation with my financial status.'

Anger drove the colour from her face, leaving it porcelain-pale. 'You think I'm after your money?'

'That I could deal with!' he retorted.

The wrath faded from Becca's face to be replaced by a baffled frown. 'I don't understand.'

'I am not my bank balance. Would being poor make me a better person? Would wearing glasses and looking geeky make me sensitive? Has it occurred to you that whenever you want to push me away you bring up the differences in our backgrounds?'

'Well, you must admit they're quite big diff...' She caught his expression and stopped.

'You make obstacles where there are none.'

She looked at him doubtfully, recognising the point he was making but not totally convinced.

'I am assuming that the main problem is that you want romantic love,' he said, and watched the colour leave her cheeks. 'That is understandable. But we are dealing with reality, here—not fairy tales.'

CHAPTER FOURTEEN

'YOU think love is a fable?'

'I think we should accept that what we have is not so bad. We give each other pleasure, and we are going to be blessed with a child we will both love. Is it adult to long for some nebulous ideal?'

You are my ideal, she thought. It was ironic that she would probably never tell him.

'I am prepared to make allowances—'

'That's good of you,' she cut back sarcastically.

'Becca, I understand your caution.'

'You do?'

'The problem is, I have no idea what is going on here. Why do you come here in the middle of the night saying you cannot marry me?'

'I didn't say I couldn't marry you.'

Eyes narrowed, he stared at her. 'I think you did. And so, incidentally, do half of my staff.'

'I said that I couldn't go through with this marriage.'

'Ah, well, that is *quite* different.' Eyes closed, he let himself fall backwards onto a large leather chesterfield. Closing his eyes, he lay sprawled there for several moments before he lifted his head and looked at her. 'I feel a great deal older than when I first saw you,' he revealed in a driven voice. 'You turn up in the middle of the night, frantic—'

'I wasn't frantic.'

'It is below zero out there, and you didn't have a coat on.'

'Okay—I was frantic.'

He arched a brow. *'Was...?'*

'It's just that you said our wedding would be something simple, and I believed you. And then at dinner, when your mother started talking about the arrangements, I realised that your definition of simple is definitely not mine!'

'Why didn't you say something then?'

'I want her to like me.'

'Which involves going along with something you hate? I see.'

'It's all right for you!' she retorted, stung by his attitude. 'I was trying to make a good impression.'

'You are marrying me, not my mother, and you have never appeared to feel the need to agree with anything I say.'

'There are plenty of people falling over themselves to do that.'

Her acid retort drew an appreciative grin from him.

'When your mother started talking about the arrangements she's made and the people who are coming she was so pleased, and she's gone to so much trouble and expense...' Becca lifted her hands in a gesture of appeal. 'How could I say anything?' she asked him.

'I'm picking up the tab for the wedding, if that makes it any easier.'

'No, it doesn't.' She rolled her eyes to the ceiling in frustration. 'I only started thinking about it properly when you had gone and I couldn't sleep.'

'You couldn't?' he echoed, sounding not unhappy about her insomnia.

'This thing is totally out of control. I mean a choir?'

'Is a choir so excessive?'

'Maybe not. But a full orchestra and a soprano being flown here from the New York Met are.'

There was a degree of caution in his deepset eyes as he scanned her pale, indignant face. 'Let me get this straight.

You still agree we need to get married? It is just the manner of that marriage that concerns you?'

Need, not *want*, she thought sadly. She knew she shouldn't let it hurt, but it did, and she was pretty damn sure it always would. She took a deep, steadying breath. Nothing she could do would turn this wedding into a joyful celebration of commitment, but she could turn it into something that wouldn't give her nightmares.

'That it scares me rigid would be closer to the truth.'

He looked baffled. 'Why are you scared?'

Her expression earnest, she struggled to explain why the lavish production this wedding had turned into was filling her with utter panic and abhorrence.

'I'm not a centre stage sort of person, Christos, and when I think of all those people looking at me…' She shuddered and pressed a protective hand to the gentle mound of her stomach. 'It's not the sort of wedding I've ever wanted. I just…'

The sudden softening of Christos's expression stopped her mid-sentence. Without warning her eyes welled with tears. For a moment she looked at the hand he extended to her—a strong hand, with long tapering fingers. She gave a gusty little sigh and reached out. She felt the familiar electric shock tingle as his warm fingers closed around hers.

'I thought all girls dreamt of the full works sort of wedding,' he said, only half teasing as he drew her towards him.

Becca eased herself onto the padded arm of the chesterfield and, shaking her head, said firmly, 'Not me. Even if this wedding had been the real thing.' She winced as the long brown fingers encircling hers tightened.

'Sorry,' Christos said, his face expressionless as he watched her rub her hand.

'It just keeps getting bigger every day,' she said, nursing

her hand against her chest. 'I mean, I thought there'd be a dozen or so guests. Do you know how many are coming?'

'Should I?'

'You obviously weren't listening at dinner,' she retorted. Her irritation didn't seem to register with him at all. From his remote expression it was hard to tell if he had even heard her.

'I must have been thinking about something else.' *Like now.*

He swallowed, the muscles in his brown throat contracting as he carried on thinking about feeling her warm soft curves beneath him, her pliant limbs winding around him, pulling him close, the sound of her fractured little gasps of pleasure hot against the skin of his neck, her hot little mouth on his skin...

He drew a deep breath. It was time to take control.

'And,' she pointed out, scowling as she recalled the elaborate arrangements Mia Carides had delighted in telling her about, 'they'll all know that I'm pregnant. I mean, it is pretty obvious.'

She looked at Christos, who looked back blankly. Maybe, she thought gloomily, he was finally seeing things from her point of view. Maybe the vision of her waddling up the aisle accounted for the beads of sweat that he was dashing from his forehead with the back of his hand.

'*Obvious?*'

The only thing obvious to Christos was that he hadn't been in control since the moment he'd laid eyes on this redheaded witch.

'Well, even if I wear a tent I'll show. They will know we wouldn't be getting married otherwise.'

She saw something flash into Christos's eyes, but before she could quite get a handle on it his dark lashes swept downwards, forming an impenetrable shield.

'Are you ashamed of being pregnant?'

Becca sprang to her feet, her eyes flashing. 'No, of course not. I'm proud!' she exclaimed.

Christos's head came up. 'And so am I.'

The wrath died from her face. Their eyes locked, dark brown on bright blue, and slowly she realised the truth.

'I believe you are!' she exclaimed.

'You sound amazed, yet children are a blessing.'

Becca doubted very much if every man in his situation would think so. But there was no doubting Christos's sincerity. 'Even children with red hair? I don't know if you've realised, but it is a possibility.'

Her apologetic manner brought a grin to his dark face.

'You know,' she said, as it suddenly hit her, 'I think you're going to be a really good dad.' Becca suddenly felt embarrassed, and had the impression that she had succeeded in surprising him.

'And husband?'

Good, bad or indifferent—he was the only one she wanted.

Her startled eyes flickered to his face. The silence stretched until Christos gave a quick hard smile and said in a dry tone, 'It would appear that the jury is still out on that one.'

'You're the one who said marriage was a gamble,' she reminded him.

'Gambling implies that you habitually lose. I prefer to think of it as a calculated risk. Not to stray too far from the point.'

Straying was a hard thing not to do, Becca reflected, when she was looking at his mouth.

'So, do I have this right? Your problem is with the ceremony, and not the marriage.'

'I suppose so—yes.' She nodded. 'It is.'

'Then I will fix it in the morning,' he promised, sliding his hand under the neckline of her silk top.

'In the morning? Are you mad? Oh, Christos, don't do that; I can't think,' she moaned, closing her eyes as his fingers moved across the tingling peak of her right breast. He stopped doing it, and she opened her eyes and snarled, 'I didn't mean it literally.'

'You are quite demented, you know—and quite delicious.' He buried his face in her hair and inhaled the sweet fragrance. 'I will sort out the wedding arrangements in the morning. I should have known better than to give my mother a free hand,' he admitted.

'But won't she be very upset?'

'Probably,' Christos agreed, not sounding at all perturbed by the prospect. 'But not as upset as I will be if you do not kiss me within the next sixty seconds.'

'I wouldn't want to upset you…'

'This is not my room.'

Becca wasn't even aware that she had voiced her sleepy confused waking thought until a voice close by observed, 'So you are finally awake.'

Blinking sleepily, she focused on the face of the man who stood a few feet away.

'Want some?' he asked, extending a mug that contained coffee towards her.

'Oh, no!' she gasped. 'I stayed the night!'

'There wasn't much night left to stay once we finally went to sleep,' he observed, raising his cup to his lips and taking a deep swallow. 'Shall I ring for more coffee?'

She raised herself on one elbow, then fell back again as the throw that was draped over her slithered down, revealing the fact that she was stark naked beneath it.

'And have someone come in here and see me? What would they think?' she gasped, horrified.

'This display of Victorian prudery after last night is somewhat hard to take.' The amusement in his eyes deepened as a dark flush spread across her fair skin. 'As for what my staff would think if they came in here—I would say it is pretty much what they're thinking now.'

'And you don't care what they think?'

'I spent the night with my fiancée and we didn't make it up the stairs. Is there something I should feel ashamed about?'

'I suppose this is normal for you. You probably make a habit of sleeping on the sofa in here when things get too urgent to make it up the stairs.'

'I have been known to spend the odd night in here,' he admitted.

'Oh, you're disgusting!' she choked.

'That's not what you said last night,' he taunted. '*Last night* you said I was pretty much marvelous—not to mention incredible and—'

Becca rolled over and pulled the cover over her head, in the process exposing a good deal of leg. 'Go away,' she said, when he lifted the throw and uncovered her tumbled curls.

'Occasionally I work through the night. I sometimes catnap here.' He laid his palm flat on the leather cushion beside her. 'Alone.'

Feeling really stupid for making such a fuss, she pushed her hair off her face and, dragging the cover with her, pulled herself into an upright position.

'What you did before we were together is none of my business.'

His lips quivered. 'That is a relief to me.'

'You're dressed,' she accused, noting for the first time the grey tailored trousers, crisp white shirt and tasteful silk tie he wore. 'You're going out somewhere? Why didn't you wake me?' she fretted. Her eyes widened. 'Erica will be frantic! We arranged to meet and I didn't leave a note or anything.'

'In reply to your first question, I am not going anywhere—*we* are.'

Becca, her face screwed up in suspicion, stared back at him. 'We are?'

'I just said so, didn't I? And in reply to your second question I did not wake you because had I done so we would not have gone anywhere.'

'Why not?'

'Do you have any idea how delicious you look when you wake up?'

'Me?'

His smouldering gaze lingered on the bare upper slopes of her breasts and he was shaken by a deep sigh. 'There is something very sensuous about the way you stretch.'

Becca, who looked at herself in the mirror every morning and thought she bore more of a resemblance to an unmade bed than this sex goddess he was describing, had no intention of pointing out his error.

'If I had woken you earlier I would have been obliged to make love to you.'

'And that would have been a bad thing?' To be considered irresistible by a man like Christos did a lot for a girl's confidence.

He responded to her provocative pout with a fierce, hungry grin. 'A very *good* thing. But we have things to do, so stop trying to distract me,' he told her sternly.

'Something more important than making love?' *I can't believe I just said that.*

Christos released his breath in a slow, sibilant hiss. 'Show a little mercy, Becca,' he pleaded throatily.

She looked back at him innocently.

'I am not made of steel,' he told her. 'Also your sister is likely to come in at any moment.' Taking the cover, which she had artfully allowed to slip down to reveal a teasing glimpse of rosy nipple, he tugged it firmly up to her chin.

Becca's eyes widened with shock as they swivelled to the door and back to Christos. 'Erica is here?'

'Yes, she is. When last seen she was in the kitchen, distracting my chef.'

'But why?'

'I require her help.'

Becca pulled her knees up to her chest. 'What is this about, Christos?'

'You want a simple marriage ceremony?' Becca nodded. 'So we are having a simple ceremony.' He glanced at the metal-banded watch on his wrist. 'In about two and a half hours.'

Shaking her head, Becca looked at him. 'This is a joke, right?'

'Wrong.'

'We can't be getting married this morning. Nobody can arrange a marriage in a few hours.'

'I am a man of resource, and my name impresses others more than it does you, it's all been arranged,' he revealed drily. 'When I use it some doors open that might otherwise stay closed,' he admitted.

'But how?'

'It has been arranged for some time. I rang my assistant, told her what I wanted, and said if she didn't get it she could look for another job.'

This tongue-in-cheek response drew a glare from Becca, who clicked her tongue in irritation. 'Will you be serious?'

'Things are looking up. Not long ago you would have taken me at my word.' His lips quirked as he angled a dark brow and wondered, 'Could it be that your opinion of me is improving?'

'Like you care what I think about you,' she mumbled.

'To be married to a wife who thinks one is in league with the devil would not be a comfortable experience.'

Was *comfortable* the best he thought their marriage could be? What a depressing thought. 'I have never thought you were evil,' she protested. 'Just opinionated, arrogant...'

'I think you should know that finishing that sentence could affect the harmony of our wedding day,' he told her solemnly.

Wedding day! She swallowed and drew a deep sighing breath. 'This isn't a wind-up? We really are getting married this morning?' It seemed impossible, but she was starting to appreciate that the word no just wasn't in Christos's vocabulary—in any of the five languages he was fluent in.

He nodded.

'You really don't let the grass grow, do you?' She gave a shaky laugh and raised her hand to her head rubbing her temples. 'What about all the people turning up for the wedding tomorrow?'

'They need not concern you.'

'See!' she cried, wagging a triumphant finger at him. 'Arrogant.'

A smile glimmered in his dark eyes. 'Do you want to have the last word or do you want to get married?' he asked, producing the black robe he had been wearing for a short time the previous evening and handing it to her.

Becca snatched it from him and did not deign to reply. 'Are you going to look away?' she asked.

Christos looked at her incredulously. 'You think there is any of you that I haven't seen?'

Flushing to the roots of her hair, and a lot of other places too, Becca straightened her shoulders, got to her feet and let the cover drop. It took a massive amount of will-power not to look at him—especially when she heard the unmistakable sound of his sharp intake of breath.

Lifting her chin defiantly, she chose to take her time to

pull on the robe. Actually, there was very little choice involved. Knowing his eyes were following her every move made her incredibly clumsy. By the time she had cinched the knot on the robe tightly her palms were damp and slick and her heart was thudding like a sledgehammer.

Fixing a bright enquiring smile on her face was almost as painful as stripping naked in front of him had been. 'Right—what next?'

Christos wasn't smiling. Neither did he look as though he was taking any pleasure from her discomfiture. The skin of his face was drawn taut, and the lines around his mouth and eyes were etched deeper by pressure that threatened to snap his control.

The touch of his smoky eyes made Becca shiver, and as the silence stretched so did the crackle of sexual tension that was an almost tangible presence in the room. When Christos finally broke the silence his voice was uneven and his accent thicker than normal.

'*Theos*, but you are beautiful!' he rasped rawly.

Before Becca could even think about responding to the remark he turned his head jerkily and, clearing his throat, opened the door.

'I'll get someone to take you to your sister.'

'We could stay here.' Her eyes widened with total horror as she heard the words spill from her lips. Clearly the connection between her vocal cords and her brain had been severed. *Talk about begging for it!*

She held her breath as he turned his head. Simple rejection she could deal with. If he said something cutting she would die of humiliation.

'I know we could, witch, but if you don't get out of here in the next twenty seconds we will miss our own wedding.'

She ran on legs that felt like jelly.

CHAPTER FIFTEEN

BECCA glared at her younger sister with frustration.

'It's no good looking at me like that,' Erica said, miming a zipping action across her lips. 'I've been sworn to secrecy. All you need to do is get ready. I've even run a bath,' she said, pushing open the door of the *en suite* bathroom.

The scent of subtle perfume and steam immediately filled the room.

'Go ahead,' Erica urged. 'Enjoy a soak. But remember,' she warned, wagging a finger at her sister, 'we're working to a strict schedule here.'

'Schedule!' Becca shrieked. 'This is a wedding, not a military exercise.'

'Well, don't blame me—I'm only following orders.'

Becca, who was starting to feel as if everyone was in on this conspiracy, flung up her hands in exasperation. 'After a lifetime of ignoring schedules you start taking notice now. Great! You do know that this is ridiculous...ludicrous?' She poked her head around the door and discovered an extremely decadent-looking sunken tub in a bathroom that was the size of a football pitch.

'It's *my* wedding—it can't be a secret from me,' she muttered crankily.

'That's not what Christos says.'

'And what he says matters?'

Erica repressed a grin. 'According to him it's on a strictly "need to know" basis, and you apparently don't need to know. You just need to look beautiful. If you want my

opinion,' she added, 'I think it's ultra-romantic. Your problem is you always like to be in control, and now you're
not.'

Pushing her open-mouthed sibling into the bathroom, she
added, 'I'd offer you some champagne,' she said, filling
her own glass from an open bottle, 'but you're not allowed,
are you?'

'You're enjoying this, aren't you?' Becca accused, lowering herself into the sweet-scented water.

Her sister's laugh came through the open door. 'What's
not to enjoy?'

Maybe she had a point, thought Becca, as the warm water lapped over her tender breasts. She sighed and felt almost mellow as some of the tension eased from between
her shoulderblades. She *did* have a problem when she
wasn't in control—which was about ninety-nine per cent
of the time around Christos.

Before she had time to get any mellower, Erica poked
her head around the door. 'Mark will be here to do your
hair in fifteen minutes. Just thought I'd let you know...'

Becca opened her mouth to protest, and then closed it
again. Did it really matter who Mark was? She had asked
for a simple wedding, but she had to make allowances for
Christos's inexperience of 'simple'.

It was an hour later when, dressed in the beaded dress
she had chosen herself, and with her hair a silken mass of
ringlets held off her face by a gold circlet of antique seed
pearls, Becca stood at the top of the sweeping staircase.

'Don't move an inch until I get Christos,' Erica
screamed, while she pelted down the stairs two at a time.
'He's got to see this!'

'This is really stupid,' Becca was muttering, when
Christos, who must have been waiting, appeared in view.

He stood at the bottom of the stairs, his eyes trained on
the slim figure at the top. Becca found his enigmatic expression hard to read.

'This is stupid,' she repeated under her breath as she began to descend. What she'd seen in the mirror had pleased her, but Christos had dated some of the most beautiful women in the world—women who were groomed and glossy. There was a limit to how much gloss a person could achieve in an hour, even with the help of the miraculous Mark and his equally talented make-up artist associate.

'No, it is not really stupid,' he retorted, shaking his head 'It is a memory I shall treasure. You look very beautiful.

The unqualified sincerity in his voice and the glow in his incredible eyes sent Becca's pulses leaping.

'Can I know where we are going now?' she asked, adding worriedly as he arranged a fur stole around her shoulders, 'I hope this isn't real fur?'

'The very best fake money can buy,' he promised. 'As to our destination—we are going to take a helicopter ride

Her astonished eyes flew to his face and he smiled enigmatically back at her. 'You're not going to tell me where are you?'

'You're catching on.'

'Help!' Becca muttered. 'I hate surprises!'

As they landed on the playing field next to the school where up until a short time ago she had worked, Becca decided she had had enough.

'Right—you tell me what's going on or I don't budge from this spot.'

'Fight! Great!' approved Erica from the seat behind 'You two are better than a trip to the cinema.'

'Shut up, Erica,' Becca said without turning her head 'Right, you,' she added, nodding her head in Christos' direction. 'Explain.'

'I'm assuming that you didn't have a discipline problem in your classroom?'

'I never had cause to raise my voice—but then I was

never teaching above the racket a helicopter makes, or teaching an extremely arrogant man.'

Amusement flickered in his eyes. 'Your mother said that your favourite place is a ruined castle.'

'Keep,' she corrected automatically. 'The castle went a long time ago. What has that got to do with anything?'

'The celebrant is meeting us there in...' he consulted his watch '...twenty minutes. Your parents, my mother and my great-aunt Theodosia will be there. Plus your very helpful sister.'

'That's me, in case you've forgotten.'

'Shut up, Erica,' Becca said again, still staring at her future husband.

'Is this small and simple enough for you? We have a table booked at the...Pheasant?...is that correct? If you wish a religious blessing at a later date that is not a problem.'

Becca nodded, her expression dazed as he mentioned the best hotel in the district. A man who could organise all this was clearly a force to be reckoned with—but then she'd already known that.

'Why are you doing this?' she asked, angling a wary look at his dark handsome face.

'Does your wedding day have to be an unpleasant memory?'

She gave a helpless shrug. 'I suppose not.'

He nodded. 'Fine. Then, if you have no more objections, can we go?'

A limo was waiting to take them to the old keep down by the river—the last visible remnant of the fortification that had been built to protect the settlement which had been here long before the present town.

As they approached the open door of the keep Becca suffered a major attack of nerves.

She started to pull back, but the hand that gripped her own tightened fractionally.

'What am I doing?' she asked out loud.

'You are getting married,' Christos replied.

His matter-of-fact tone had a calming effect on Becca.

'Your mother said you used to come here when you were a child and pretend to be a princess.'

'You must have been riveted.'

Christos paused and allowed Erica to enter the room before them. 'And now you look like a queen.'

Before Becca could do anything but stare at him he was drawing her inside. She blinked as she took in the transformation which had been wrought on the simple room with its lofty rafters and exposed stone walls.

The transformation had been brought about mainly by filling every available space with flowers. Hundreds and thousands of sweet-smelling flowers.

The guests who were seated in a semi-circle at the far end of the room rose as they entered. With the exception of the woman with bright beady eyes, wearing pearls looped again and again around her thin wrinkled neck, they were all familiar faces. Christos's mother and her parents.

The celebrant smiled encouragingly as they approached.

Becca took a deep breath and thought, *This is it.* With a smile she stepped forward.

The ceremony had gone like a dream. The celebratory meal later was another matter.

'What's wrong?' Christos asked.

'You can't come in here!' she exclaimed, pulling a fresh tissue from the box provided.

'Why?'

'It says "Ladies' Room" on the door for a reason.'

'I'm not going until you tell me what is wrong,' he countered. 'It was something Theodosia said, wasn't it?'

'She hates me,' Becca said, biting back a sob. 'Sorry,' she added with a grimace. 'Hormones.'

'Of course she doesn't hate you! What exactly did she say?'

'She asked me how far gone I was. I said f...four months, and she looked at me and said I'm far too big for four months. She obviously thinks I'm trying to pass off someone else's baby as yours.' She shook her head. 'I'm not!'

'Hush,' Christos said, laying his hands on her shoulders. 'I'm sure she thinks nothing of the sort—and does it even matter what she thinks?'

'She thinks,' came a loud voice from behind a stall door, 'that twins run in this family. In my opinion you're big, because you're carrying two Carides. Now, will you two go away and leave an old lady some privacy?'

'Twins?' Becca gulped. 'Is that possible, do you think?'

'I don't know,' Christos admitted. 'We need to find out. But now I think we should join the party,' he said, taking her hand.

Despite this advice, when they did join the others Christos did not seem in a party mood. As Becca herself was feeling pretty stunned by the possibility that she might be carrying two babies she could appreciate his mood.

As they were driven back to the helicopter he remained withdrawn and aloof. It was only when the car came to a halt he turned to her.

'Do you regret marrying me?'

Startled by the question, Becca responded without thinking. 'No, I don't.'

His intense expression didn't alter, but she saw something flicker in the back of his dark eyes at her response.

'You didn't marry me because I threatened to contest your custody, did you, Becca?'

Becca shook her head.

'Then why?'

'Maybe I thought you were right.' She looked at his mouth and thought of it against her skin. 'Maybe,' she admitted huskily, 'I think that a baby needs both parents too.'

'And maybe,' he suggested silkily, 'you didn't hate the idea of being married to me as much as you suggested?'

Her eyes lowered. 'I suppose there are some benefits to being married to you.'

He took her chin in his hand and lifted her face to his. 'And as soon as we get back to the house I will show you some of them,' he promised, in a sensuous growl that made her shiver with anticipation. 'But first I will delay our flight for twenty-four hours.'

'Flight?'

'We are going to Venice for our honeymoon. But first I think that after what Aunt Theodosia said we should make a visit to your doctor.'

CHAPTER SIXTEEN

FROM the moment the doctor said cheerfully, 'Yes—definitely two heartbeats there,' Becca's life changed.

She had no problem with Christos being protective. In fact for five minutes she actually thought it might be quite nice to be spoiled a little and to feel cherished. But she swiftly learned that the advantages were outweighed by the disadvantages.

The news that she was carrying two babies brought out the autocratic side of Christos's nature with a vengeance! To Becca's initial amusement, and then her increasing dismay, he went totally overboard and acted as though a puff of wind was going to damage her.

The first thing he did was cancel their honeymoon plans for Venice. But, since almost overnight Christos appeared to have stopped looking at her as though she was a sexually desirable female, maybe, Becca reflected bitterly, that was not such a bad thing.

She told herself that a lot of men didn't find pregnant women sexually attractive, and that things would go back to how they had been after the babies were born. But sometimes she secretly wondered if this was wishful thinking on her part.

Things might have been easier to bear if she had gone to Greece with him as they had originally planned, but he had decreed that impossible.

'The stress of the journey...the heat,' he said, looking astonished that she should even suggest it. 'There would be no network of support from close family, and that is very important at a time like this.'

'What would you know about *a time like this*?' she was goaded into retorting childishly.

'I am learning.' The expression on his face said loud and clear that she should be too. 'No flitting back and forth to Greece. It is out of the question.'

Despite her continued protests, and her obstetrician saying that as far as he was concerned she could fly up until the last weeks of her pregnancy, Christos remained immovable on the subject. And, as he was in the middle of delicate negotiations which required him to be not just in Athens but several other European locations, Becca was frequently left alone at home in London.

She tried to put a brave face on it. When he cursed the timing and asked if she was lonely she lied and told him she enjoyed the time alone. In reality she missed him more than she would have thought possible. Far from becoming part of his life, as she had hoped, she felt further away from him than ever.

Several times when he *was* there she almost lost her temper when he remonstrated with her for doing something he considered too physically taxing—there was very little, it seemed to her, that he *didn't* consider too taxing—but each time she bit her tongue and kept quiet.

She knew that his attitude stemmed from a deep-seated fear that history would repeat itself, and she couldn't be mad with the man for worrying about the health of their babies. But understanding his motivation didn't stop her wanting to take a swing at him when she accidentally learnt that the staff had instructions to spy on her and report to him if she did anything reckless—like opening a packet of biscuits!

When she had challenged him about this he had not displayed any repentance. 'Do not be paranoid, Becca. It is not a question of *spying*,' he had retorted, his lips spasming in distaste at the emotive terminology. 'I simply need to

know that in my absence you are taking care of yourself.'
He'd angled a questioning brow. 'Of course if you'd agreed
to have a maternity nurse live in, as I suggested—'

'I am pregnant—not sick!' Becca had flared back, even
more exasperated than the last time he had tabled this ridiculous notion. 'As I told you last time, when you came
up with that totally daft idea, I do *not* need a keeper, a
nurse, or staff spying on me.'

Christos hadn't pressed the idea, but she had come away
feeling irrationally guilty that she was the cause of the lines
of strain around his eyes, and it did not feel like a triumph.

Thirty-six weeks into her pregnancy Christos returned un-
expectedly, looking exhausted after a three-night absence,
and casually announced that he had taken a sabbatical and
would not be leaving her side again until some time after
the birth.

'Can you do that?' she wondered, thinking of the awe-
some responsibilities he shouldered.

'I can do anything I wish,' he replied, sounding
astounded that she should think otherwise. A hard expression filtered into his eyes as he added, 'Afraid having me
around will cramp your style?'

Becca stared at him, not understanding the peculiar inflection in his voice. Maybe the thought of months of do-
mestic bliss was responsible for his cranky mood. *'Style?'*
she echoed with a derisive hoot. 'What style? A ten-ton
truck has more style than I do,' she reflected as she eased
her bulk into a chair.

'You look just as an expectant mother should.' The tact-
ful response caused her to smile as she met his eyes.
'Though a little tired.'

'For that matter, so do you,' Becca retorted, noting the
grey tinge under his tan and the lines of strain bracketing

his mouth. 'I'm carrying a bit of extra weight—what's your excuse? You know what I think your problem is, Christos?'

She was trying to figure out why her innocuous remark should cause him to stiffen and look at her so oddly when he prompted in a harsh, almost driven voice, 'What is my problem, then?'

'You're a total workaholic.'

For some reason she couldn't fathom he found her response amusing.

'It's true,' she protested. 'You are.'

She looked at him, wanting to rub away the frown lines from between his eyes. But she no longer thought it was a coincidence that every time she initiated physical contact he made some excuse and left the room, so she repressed her impulse rather than risk the pain of rejection.

'Will you be glad to have me around?' he asked, studying her face with an intensity she found unnerving.

'Of course.' The sheer frustration of being unable to tell him how glad she was made Becca's guarded response emerge sounding stilted.

'Or maybe you have got used to having the place to yourself?' he suggested.

'It will take some adjusting to,' Becca admitted.

'You won't be alone for much longer,' Christos observed, his strong dark features clenched taut as he looked at her belly.

'I hope not. I feel as though this has been the longest pregnancy in history,' she sighed.

When he left to shower and change before a late dinner, Becca dashed down to the kitchen and conspired with the very compliant chef to produce all the things Christos liked best for their meal together.

Sitting there later, looking at her plate, Becca wondered how she could have been so pathetically eager to please him—Christos was so 'glad' to be home that he had dashed away at the first half-legitimate pretence.

They had barely sat down when his mobile had rung.

'Kyria…?'

Becca looked up from her moody contemplation of her untouched food and forced a smile for the benefit of Spyros, the butler.

'Would you like some dessert? A little of the lemon pudding you like so much, kyria…?' he suggested tentatively.

Becca shook her head. 'No, thanks. It doesn't look as though Christos will be home. Say sorry to Fabien for me, will you? And tell him the food was delicious, as usual.'

Upstairs, she showered and changed and went to bed, planning the things she was going to say to Christos when he finally deigned to come home.

She re-ran in her head the events that had led to her yelling recklessly as he had walked out of the door, 'Well, if you walk out now don't expect me to be here when you get back!'

The expression on his face as he had swung back, his dark eyes narrowed to slits, even now had the power to make her shiver. 'Do not make childish threats you have no intention of following through.'

'How do you know I won't walk out?'

'If I didn't know it was your hormones talking I would seriously worry about your mental health.' He had narrowed his dark eyes on her flushed face and added incredulously, 'You don't actually think that I would allow you to leave, do you?'

'You wouldn't notice if I wasn't here,' she'd flung back childishly.

Christos, his expression taut and irritated, had passed a hand across his eyes. 'We will talk when I get back.'

'Maybe I won't want to talk then.'

Going over it in her head, she recognised that her sulky

retort hadn't been her finest hour—but how was she supposed to behave? Her husband had only just told her he was never going to leave her side, and then straight off had dropped everything because the cousin he loathed had a problem only he could sort out.

Was she being totally paranoid, or did that sound slightly less plausible than world peace?

Later that night, slipping beneath the silken sheets of the bed they shared—or were meant to—she realised how often Christos used the excuse of not wanting to wake her for sleeping on the sofa in the dressing room.

Erotic recollections of past times were generally the only thing she had to keep her warm at night. And if there had been something other than glorious head-banging sex to bind them—at least on his side—Becca might not have been haunted by the possibility that a highly sexed man like Christos was satisfying his hunger elsewhere.

She sat up suddenly, her face a mask of resolution as she sniffed and brushed the tears of self-pity from her cheeks. Maybe it was time to find out one way or the other if her anxieties were founded!

And if they are…?

Becca shook her head in silent denial. She didn't want to think about what she would do if they were.

Her fingers trembled as she dialled Alex's number. The phone was picked up almost immediately—which in other circumstances might have struck her as strange at two in the morning.

'Sally, this is Becca. I'm really sorry to disturb you, but could I speak to Christos?'

There was a short pause, and what might have been a sniff, before the other woman replied, 'I'm sorry, Becca. He isn't here.'

He'd lied…!

Why am I so shocked? she asked herself?

'Becca? Are you there? He shou—'

The phone dropped from her nerveless fingers onto the carpet. She pressed her hand across her mouth and let out a strangled cry of utter misery from her aching throat.

She had thought it would be better to know one way or the other. Now she knew how wrong she had been! She knew she ought to be feeling something—she wasn't sure what, but *something*.

Instead she just felt strangely numb and unnaturally calm as she set about packing a bag, her actions slow and methodical as she moved around the room, shaking out a crease or smoothing a fold.

'Inevitable, really,' she said to the empty room. 'He never loved me—never even pretended to.' She gave a dry-eyed sniff and bit down hard on her trembling lip.

But he had promised to be faithful, and he had broken that promise. She couldn't live with his infidelity—not even for the sake of her unborn babies.

She sat on the end of the bed and formulated her plans. She would stay with her mum and dad until the present tenant's lease on her cottage ran out, in six months' time. Getting her job back was unfortunately not an option but if she was lucky she might get some supply work.

Her lip quivered and she started to cry. She was still crying two hours later when, totally exhausted by the emotional outpouring, she fell into a deep, dreamless sleep.

When she awoke the first thing she saw was Christos's face, inches from her own. Her initial sleepy pleasure at seeing him was quickly replaced by a potent mix of anger and loss—immense, incapacitating loss.

Carefully, without taking her eyes from his sleeping face, she edged her body away from his and levered herself with utmost care off the bed. She stood there holding her breath when he stirred and murmured in his sleep, but after a moment his breathing became even and heavy again.

Like her, he had fallen asleep wearing his clothes—the same clothes he had left the house in the previous night. She looked down at him, the expression on her face an accurate reflection of the confusing mixture of emotions that were tearing her in disparate directions.

A terrible surge of longing welled up in her as she gazed down. She tried to block the images that entered her head. Images of him over her, the muscles in his powerful shoulders and arms bunched with tension as his lean, streamlined body, slick with sweat, slid... She inhaled sharply, sucking in air through flared nostrils as she fought to free herself of the erotic memories.

For a moment she had almost followed the voice in her head that told her it would be all right to lie down beside him, to feel the strength of his long, lean body next to her for the last time.

Have you no pride, woman? she asked herself.

Holding back the tears, Becca stumbled towards the door, not trusting herself to be in the same room as him. In the hallway she leant against the wall and, eyes closed, took several deep, restorative breaths.

The world is full of cheating men; you married one—get over it, she told herself. Feeling not even slightly over it, and doubting she ever would, she raked her fingers through her disordered curls. You have some choices to make, she told herself, and remembered the bag she had packed the previous night, wondering if she could risk going back in to get it.

'Kyria...?'

Becca opened her eyes and found the normally impassive butler looking at her with some concern.

'You are well?'

She nodded. 'Just getting my breath. Is something wrong?' *Apart from my life being messed up beyond belief.*

He glance swivelled pointedly towards the bedroom door. 'Is—?'

'He's asleep,' Becca cut in quickly. 'We probably shouldn't disturb him. Can I help?'

'There is a visitor,' the butler explained hesitantly, quite clearly not convinced by her attempt to appear normal.

'Well, you'll have to tell them that Christos is not available just now.'

'The visitor is asking for you, *kyria*...'

Something in the man's strange manner sent a premonitory shudder through her body and she asked, 'Just who is this visitor?'

'It is Miss Karas. She was...'

'She was engaged to my husband,' Becca inserted, in a calm voice that gave no hint of the fact that she felt as though she was dying inside.

Her thoughts were racing. Could this be the answer to the question she had not dared ask herself yet? Was Melina Karas the woman Christos had spent last night with? And heaven knew how many other nights when he was allegedly away on business?

'She is waiting?'

'It was difficult to stop her, *kyria*. She was insistent. I think perhaps I should waken Mr Carides—' he began doubtfully.

Becca straightened her shoulders decisively. 'No, I'll deal with this.'

CHAPTER SEVENTEEN

THE woman in the small salon turned as Becca entered, her demeanour, and the edge of condescension in her smile as she looked Becca up and down very much that of the mistress of the house and not the visitor.

Becca returned the scrutiny of those almond-shaped eyes, their exotic brilliance enhanced by expertly applied colour, with a steadiness that seemed to unnerve the other woman slightly.

'You don't know who I am—'

'Yes,' Becca cut in. 'I do.'

'Why don't you sit down?' the older woman suggested, still in the manner of a gracious, concerned hostess.

Becca, who needed quite badly to sit down, immediately decided she'd die before she did so now. The sympathy and consideration of her husband's mistress was more of a salt-in-the-wound situation than she was prepared to tolerate.

If she was his mistress?

Was this really the sort of woman Christos would be unable to live without? For the first time Becca questioned her own conviction as she observed the malicious light shining in the dark beauty's eyes.

Christos was normally such an instinctively good judge of character, but love had quite obviously dimmed his normal powers of perception. Becca could tell at a glance that this woman, despite her stunning looks, was cold and shallow. Of course she would still have hated her with a vengeance even if she had turned out to be delightful and warm.

Becca lifted her chin and shook her head, a frown forming between her brows as she studied her beautiful visitor.

'I've seen you before, haven't I?'

She frowned as she made the mental connection between this tall, elegant and very beautiful brunette in her home and the woman who had offered her opinion on fluffy bunnies versus cartoon cats when it came to mobiles for babies' cots.

'You were in the shop—and then in the café I went to the other day.' Comprehension flickered in her eyes. 'And it wasn't a coincidence, was it? You were following me!' she accused in horror.

'I admit I was curious,' the other woman responded, with a careless shrug of her narrow shoulders. 'Curious to see what sort of woman had trapped Christos into marriage.'

'I didn't trap Christos into anything.'

'Of course you did. But that really doesn't matter now,' she conceded with a generous smile. 'At first I admit I was angry with you—for taking advantage when he was vulnerable. But then I realised that you were clearly besotted with him and therefore not entirely to blame for your actions. You know, of course, that Christos loves *me*?'

A few minutes earlier this statement would have made Becca want to crawl away into a corner and lick her wounds. She had walked into the room prepared to see the woman Christos preferred to her, his wife. The woman who could make him happy.

But then, as she had listened to this incredibly beautiful creature, who was everything Becca was not, she'd become more and more convinced that she wasn't looking at that woman.

This woman could never make Christos happy. She could never love him the way he deserved to be loved! She was hard, selfish and mean. Not the most objective conclusion in the world, but Becca's gut instincts told her she was right on this one.

Becca lifted her chin and smiled. 'He married me.'

The other woman's smile wavered slightly as this quietly confident response threw her off-balance. 'I feel sorry for you.'

'Because Christos married me?' Becca shook her head. 'I don't think so,' she mused. 'I think you're actually as jealous as hell of me.'

A unattractive mottled tide of angry colour rose up Melina's neck as the remark found its intended target. 'His family will never accept you. You'll always be an outsider!' she hissed.

'And what would you know about it?'

'We've been seeing each other for months!' she yelled shrilly. With a triumphant grin she pulled out a notebook from her bag and began to flick through the pages. 'Athens, Rome, Paris—I have all the dates and hotels.'

Watching her, it dawned on Becca that her visitor was far from stable. She glanced towards the door. 'My husband's travel arrangements are not a secret.'

'And last night he was with me.' She saw the colour fade from Becca's face and smiled. *'All night,'* she emphasised with malice. 'And look at yourself,' she invited with a sneer. 'Do you honestly blame him? You look as though you slept in those clothes.'

Before Becca could confirm that she had, the door burst open and Christos, who had definitely slept in his, stood there. His expression belligerent, he locked his dark explosive eyes with Becca's. Eyes still glued to hers, he stepped inside and, after slamming the door behind him, tipped the contents of the suitcase she had so carefully packed the previous night over the floor. The bag followed it.

'What the hell does this mean?' he demanded.

'It means you'll have to pick them up, because when I

get down it takes a crane to get me up again.' She patted her distended belly and sighed.

Her response threw him slightly. 'If you think you are going anywhere without me—*Theos. Melina...?*' He looked from one woman to the other. 'What the hell are you doing here?'

Melina tore her startled glance from the pile of clothes on the floor and lifted her melting eyes to Christos's face.

Christos's response to her passionate flood of Greek was a cold terse instruction. 'Speak English in front of my wife.' He turned his head to Becca. 'Melina appears to think that she has saved me the painful task of *telling you*.' He turned back to the other woman. 'Telling her what, exactly, Melina?'

His voice was filled with icy disdain. This was Christos at his most cold and cutting. Becca almost started to feel sorry for the other woman.

Melina looked flustered, and gave a light laugh. 'That we still love one another, darling. That our breaking up was just a silly mistake. It's understandable that you didn't want to say anything, with her being pregnant.' Her thin lips formed a *moue* of pained distaste as she glanced at Becca's distended waistline.

'I take it that you had no such qualms?' Christos suggested drily.

If Becca or the babies suffered because of this he would personally strangle the woman. Even if the balance of her mind was quite definitely seriously disturbed!

'I thought she deserved to know.'

This pious statement wrenched a strangled expletive from a grim-looking Christos.

'I love you, Christos.'

'Then I can live without your brand of love.' His eyes flickered towards Becca. 'Are you okay?'

'That would be overstating it,' Becca admitted. 'But I'm hanging in there, fighting.'

'She's in denial,' said Melina compassionately.

Christos gave her a frowning, impatient glance. 'She has nothing to be in denial about. I don't love you and I never did.'

Melina flinched, then shook her head. Her eyes held a feral gleam of determination as she gazed at him. 'You don't mean that. We are meant to be together. You're only being like this because of her!' she hissed, throwing a malevolent glance towards Becca.

Intercepting that look, Christos moved to interpose his body protectively between that of his wife and his ex.

As Melina advanced towards him Christos held up his hands and shook his head. Something in his manner must have finally pierced the fantasy she had constructed, because Melina stopped dead, the colour draining from her face.

Becca looked away, embarrassed, as her rival quivered. 'But you love me.'

'I am married—and even if I wasn't I have no feelings for you.'

The brutally honest response drew a sharp gasp from Melina.

'I think you should leave,' Christos said, and warned in the same devastating soft voice, 'If you come anywhere near my family again there will be consequences, Melina.' He picked up the phone.

Becca, who was watching him, had no doubt he meant it. And it seemed from the way Melina straightened her shoulders and picked up her designer bag that she believed him too.

'I'll call you a cab.'

'Don't bother,' Melina snapped. 'I know my way out.' At the door she turned back, and her smile as she looked at Becca was vicious. 'Tell her where you were last night if you weren't with me, Christos.'

The door slammed and her parting shot hung in the air between them.

Becca sat down heavily on the sofa. After looking down at her glossy bowed head for a moment, Christos released a strong expletive and fell onto his knees beside her.

He lifted a gentle hand to her cheek and Becca looked back at him blankly, still trying to make sense of what had just happened.

'I'm really sorry you had to go through that. I had no idea she'd pull a stunt like that,' he admitted, with a self-recriminatory grimace as their eyes meshed. 'You coped remarkably well, you know.'

Becca stilled, then with an ironic laugh turned her head away. 'You thought that was coping?' She swallowed and shook her head. 'I thought you were having an affair, Christos.' She turned back and caught a look of shocked devastation on his handsome face that could not have been feigned.

'You thought I was having an affair?' She nodded and he shook his dark head. 'I don't know what to say.'

'*No, I'm not* would be good…' She paused. 'If it's true?' she added huskily.

He flinched as if she had struck him. '*If?*' he echoed hoarsely. 'If?' he said again, then, visibly restraining himself, sucked in air through flared nostrils. 'That was why you packed the bag? You were going to leave me? You were serious last night?'

'Yes… No… I don't know,' she admitted, bowing her head.

Christos looked at the top of her glossy head for a long time before he spoke. 'I could not bear to lose you.'

Her head lifted. His face was filled with the same depth of aching sincerity and pain she had heard in his voice.

This is about the babies, she cautioned her hopeful heart. But of course it didn't listen.

'And I couldn't bear to think of you making love to someone else,' she admitted bluntly.

'How could you think such a thing?'

She stared at him. 'Well you haven't been making love to *me* have you?' She watched a telltale flush of colour run up under his olive-toned skin and her heart sank.

The skin was drawn tight across his face, lending stark prominence to each perfect contour and angle as he said, 'I've been worried about the babies.'

'Don't use them as an excuse,' she recommended, in no mood at that moment to be sympathetic to his concerns. 'I may be the size of a small mountain now,' she admitted, with a rueful glance down at her girth, 'but I wasn't when you stopped touching me,' she reminded him bitterly. 'Why don't you just admit you can't stand the sight of me?' she yelled, clamping a hand over her mouth to contain the self-pitying sob in her throat.

He looked at her incredulously. 'Is that what you think?'

'It's what I know,' she contended stubbornly.

'Theos!' He lifted both hands and dragged them through his already disordered dark hair. When his hands fell back to his sides Becca saw he was laughing.

Her chest swelled with indignation. 'You think this is funny!' she shrieked, and seriously considered hitting him.

Christos stopped laughing and suddenly grabbed her by the shoulders. There was no trace of the humour that had offended her in his face as he leaned in close to her.

'No,' he said as she lowered her chin. 'Look at me, *pethu mou.*'

Her heart beating very fast, Becca did as he demanded—and when his fierce gaze locked with hers what she saw glittering in his fabulous eyes made her heart beat even faster.

'I stopped touching you because I was afraid.'

'I…I don't understand,' she faltered.

'Two babies…'

At that point Becca lost her temper with him. 'Do you think I would do or encourage *you* to do anything that would harm the babies?' she demanded indignantly. 'I know your mother had a hard time, and things went badly, but I'm not your mother. In fact I'm not a mother at all yet. And when I am I'd like to feel like a woman too. But at the moment I can't ever imagine…'

Her emotional tirade ran out of impetus at about the same time she ran out of breath. Tears flowing freely down her face, she sat there, her bosom heaving as she gasped for air.

'Feel like a woman? Of course you're a woman—a warm, desirable woman. This is not about me not finding you attractive.'

His response had soothed her feelings slightly, but her eyes still held hostility as she asked, 'Then what is it about?'

'Do you have any idea how much higher the maternal mortality rate is with multiple births?' he demanded. When she shook her head he said grimly, 'I do.'

'If a pregnancy has ever been more carefully monitored than mine, I have yet to hear about it,' she retorted grimly.

'I have always prided myself on my self-control, but when I touch you…' A deep sigh lifted his chest and his lips twisted in a self-derisory grimace. 'You must admit that our lovemaking was never tame, *pethu mou*.' The gentle flush that ran up her neck until her face was bathed in colour brought a wicked glint to his eyes.

Becca realised how much she had missed that glint.

'I have a vague recollection,' she admitted huskily. She turned her exasperated glare on him. 'Fair enough, you're worried about sex—but that doesn't mean you can't hug me, or show me a little bit of affection or...'

'But you never appeared to need—'

'I didn't need what?' she asked, when he stopped mid-sentence.

'Me.'

Becca looked at him in staggered silence. That Christos could feel any form of insecurity about her needing him had never even crossed her mind.

'You appeared to enjoy the time we spent apart. You never displayed any sign of missing me,' he recalled accusingly. 'I felt...' He swallowed. 'I felt at times irrelevant,' he admitted.

The concept of Christos Carides ever being *irrelevant* made her blink. It had never occurred to her that he was capable of feeling this sort of insecurity.

'You're the least irrelevant person I have ever met, Christos.'

'What if I lost control and—?'

'*Rubbish!*'

He looked at her in startled enquiry and Becca spelt out her meaning.

'Christos, you could never hurt me.' She shook her head to emphasise her total conviction. 'You're a passionate lover, not some sort of selfish brute, and I won't have you think about yourself that way.'

Before he had a chance to respond she took his face between her hands and pressed her mouth to his. For a moment there was no response, and then a deep sigh vibrated through him and he was kissing her back, with a tenderness that went bone-deep.

When they broke apart Christos looked as shaken as Becca felt.

He blotted a tear that was running down her cheek. 'It has been hell not to touch you,' he confessed huskily.

Tell me about it, Becca thought, and sniffed.

'But with us it never stops with a touch, does it?' There was fascination in his eyes as he raised a hand to her burnished curls. 'I catch fire when I touch you.'

It seemed to a mesmerised Becca that there was a flame deep in his eyes as he looked at her. 'There's nothing wrong with a bit of combustion.' She slanted him a sultry look from under the sweep of her lashes and confided huskily, 'I rather enjoy it.'

'You know that my twin brother was stillborn?'

The fear she saw lurking in his eyes made her heart ache with empathy. 'Our babies are healthy, Christos.' She pressed her hands to her belly. 'Feel, if you don't believe me. They're right here.'

He looked startled for a moment. Then his strong, masculine features relaxed into an excited, almost boyish smile of anticipation as he raised his hand. He still hesitated. 'May I...?'

Becca took his hand and pressed it to her stomach.

His eyes widened as he felt the vigorous movement within. 'Do they do that all the time?' he asked in an awed whisper.

'Pretty much,' she confirmed. 'So, you see, they are a tough pair.'

His eyes blazing, he took her small hand and pressed it to his lips. 'And they will remain that way,' he promised.

'Of course they will.' Becca studied his face, trying to understand the source of the tension that was emanating from him.

'After I was born my mother became ill. Obviously I have no memory of the time, and it is not spoken of, but children hear things...'

Becca nodded. She was a teacher—she was only too aware of children's ability to hear things they weren't meant to.

'And they make an impression…stay with the child.'

Clearly whatever he was about to tell her had made an impression on the young Christos. Becca waited, knowing that this wasn't the time to rush him, even though the anguish in his face made her want to weep with frustration because she wasn't able to stop him hurting.

'After the trauma of the birth and…' he paused slightly before he said the name of the brother he had never known. 'Vasilis's death, my mother suffered from a form of what I assume would be called post-natal depression today. These things were not so readily recognised then.

'For a long time,' he continued, 'she was hard to reach. My parents' marriage suffered greatly. She became angry and resentful, and, in her grief she came to believe that it was my father's fault that my brother died.'

'People need someone to blame.'

He nodded agreement. 'She accused him of putting his pleasure first and killing her baby.'

'Oh, the poor man!' Becca exclaimed. 'And how your mother must have regretted it later.'

'I'm sure she did,' Christos agreed. 'But this tragedy cast a shadow over my parents' marriage for many years. That, and the fact that the birth left her unable to have more children. If you ever said such a thing to me, Becca…' He shook his head and swallowed.

Becca knew she would never forget the terrible haunted light in his eyes as he looked at her. 'For an intelligent man you are pretty dim—do you know that?' she told him huskily.

To be called dim was obviously a new experience for Christos, who looked so astonished she almost laughed.

'If you had these worries why didn't you share them with me?'

A bemused frown formed between his dark brows. *'Share…?'*

This time she did laugh. 'Married people do—and we are married, you know.'

'Are we?' His glance slid significantly to the clothes on the floor. 'But you were going to leave me.'

'When I rang Alex's last night you weren't there.'

'You rang...?' He looked aghast, which a short time ago Becca would have translated as guilty, but now she was seeing things more clearly.

'I kind of put two and two together, as you do...' she admitted, trying to block that devastating moment from her memory. 'Now I realise I was being stupid. If you were going to cheat you'd tell me. You're much too up-front to sneak around.' And she was pretty sure that if he had it would not have been with Melina, who had a smile like a snake and was ever so slightly mad.

'Melina was stalking me, you know.'

This casual revelation caused Christos to stop grinding his teeth and stare at her.

'She was what?' he exclaimed, and Becca went on the explain about the shop and the café.

Christos rubbed his jaw and looked shaken and angry. 'I wish you'd told me.'

'I didn't know she was your ex-fiancée when I saw her.' Her eyes slid from his. '*Were* you at Melina's place last night?'

His jaw tightened. 'Yes. But not doing what you think.'

Her eyes flew to his face. 'You don't know what I think,' she protested.

'You will have no argument from me on that score,' he retorted, with feeling. 'Your thought processes remain a total mystery to me. Am I meant to take it as a *compliment* that you think I will be ''up-front'' when I choose to cheat on you?' One dark brow lifted as he enquired with heavy irony, 'With my cheating apparently being taken as some sort of given? *Theos!*' he breathed. 'I never know what you're going to say next.'

'I didn't—'

'No,' he said cutting across her with an impatient movement of his hand. 'For the sake of my sanity I think it best you don't go there.' He drew a deep breath. 'I was telling you about last night.'

'You don't have to.'

He studied her face in silence for a moment. 'Oh, I think I do. Sally has suspected for a few weeks that Alex has resumed his affair with Melina—'

'Melina and Alex!' Becca gasped.

Christos nodded. 'Well, I'm not sure that it can be termed an ''affair''—but Alex could never resist the opportunity to get one over on me—and Melina was bitter when I broke off our engagement.'

Becca lifted a hand to his cheek. '*You* broke off the engagement? But I thought…'

Christos's dark gaze moved across her flushed face. 'I hardly dare ask,' he revealed drily, 'but what did you think, *yineka mou*?'

'I thought that she dumped you, and you slept with me on the rebound.'

His dark brows lifted as an expression of incredulity spread across his face. 'Your readiness to believe that other women are as ready to reject me as you does wonders for my fragile ego. And this extraordinary conclusion was based on what evidence, exactly?'

'Imagination and jealousy.' Easy to recognise in retrospect, but not at the time.

'My engagement to Melina was over almost before it began. It never was a planned thing,' he revealed. 'She got drunk at her parents' anniversary party and had her father announce to the entire world that we were engaged. I should have stopped it then. But I thought, Why not…?'

His shoulders lifted in an expressive shrug, and his voice contained a large dose of self-derision as he explained his reasoning.

'We had a lot in common, and we'd had an on-off thing for some years...' he admitted. 'I wanted a family. It was not difficult to convince myself that it would be enough of a marriage for me. You see, in my defence, at that point in my life I had never seen a particular redhead. So I didn't know how much better than *all right* and *workable* things could be.'

Becca's eyes misted with emotional tears as she brought his hand to her face.

'I started to regret it straight away,' he admitted.

'What did she do when you called it off?'

'She knew I was coming over to return her keys, so she arranged a little...floorshow. Which involved Alex and her with very few clothes and a rug.'

Becca gasped, trying hard not to imagine the scene he described. 'And you walked in?'

He nodded, amused by her shocked expression.

'What did you do?'

'Nothing.'

Becca stared at him. *'Nothing?'* she echoed in a bemused voice. 'That doesn't seem very in character.'

'Why should I have done anything when I didn't give a damn? It may interest you to know that five minutes after I'd met you—maybe less—I punched my cousin on the nose. Twice, actually.'

'Why?'

'Because I thought he had done to you what he did to Erica.'

Choking back an emotional sob, Becca flung her arms around his neck and kissed him several times, interspersing the kisses with fervent thank-yous. 'Not,' she added when she eventually drew back, 'that I approve of violence.'

'Of course not,' he concurred gravely.

'But Alex is the most horrible man.'

'No arguments there.'

'It's poor Sally I feel for.'

Christos nodded. 'A nice girl—she deserves a lot better than my cousin. Last night when she confronted him he apparently admitted that he was spending the night with Melina. When she rang me she was in a terrible state. She begged me to use my influence…said if I told Melina to leave him alone she would. I thought that was unlikely, but she was so desperate that I went round there to remind my cousin that he had wife and a baby at home.'

'Just as Melina planned you would.'

'You caught on to that faster than I did,' he admitted, a glint of startled admiration in his dark eyes as they met her own. 'When I got there Alex was very drunk,' he recalled. 'But he was not actually the problem.'

'It was *you* Melina was after.'

'I will not go into details,' he said, his lips twisting into a grimace of fastidious distaste as he recalled the previous evening, 'but when I said thanks, but no thanks, she became…*unpleasant*.' Only his very quick reflexes had stopped her raking his face with her nails.

Becca, who had seen for herself how 'unpleasant' Melina could be, could imagine how horrendous it must have been. 'You got Alex home?'

Christos nodded. 'Eventually—and I think I got through to him.'

'You did?'

Christos nodded. 'I told him what the rumour mill says his father-in-law did to a guy who tried to embezzle from him. I think it made an impression. The one thing that Carl cares about more than making money is his daughter.'

'I know I shouldn't have jumped to conclusions,' Becca admitted, her eyes sliding guiltily from his.

'I should have appreciated how it looked from your point of view.'

Sighing with pleasure as she felt the touch of his fingers in her hair, Becca mused thoughtfully, 'I suppose it makes you a little insecure, loving someone so much when you know they don't love you back.'

The hand that had been stroking her hair stilled. 'You love me?'

For a split second she considered denying it, and then thought—What the hell? It wasn't as if she was going to be able to hide it for ever.

There was a hint of defiance in her face as she levelled her eyes with his. 'So what if I love you? It doesn't change anything.'

'You being in love with me doesn't change anything?' He stared at her as if she was totally insane. 'The hell it doesn't!' he growled, a split second before his mouth came down on hers, hard and hungry.

When he lifted his head and put her carefully from him, as though she was breakable, they were both breathing hard.

If this is a dream I definitely don't want to wake up, she thought, looking at his lean, dark face with eyes that glowed with love. 'I take it you don't mind about…you know…?'

'Mind?' He gave a grin of fierce relief, the tension visibly seeping from his body. 'My dear, delicious lunatic— why should I mind my wife loving me?'

Becca blinked up at him.

'You look like a confused baby owl,' he told her lovingly.

'Men do not fall in love with confused owls of any age.'

He gave a complacent laugh and, after running a loving hand over her stomach, let it remain there. 'I've been crazy in love with you from the first moment I laid eyes on that red head of yours. I knew I couldn't let you get away from me.'

Becca started to shake. 'You only married me because I was pregnant!' she protested weakly.

'I married you because I can't live without you,' Christos corrected, nibbling his way reverently along the smooth curve of her shoulder.

'And it didn't occur to you to tell me?' she moaned, laying her head against his chest and thinking of all the miserable nights she had spent.

'Now, why am I thinking pot, black and kettle?' he teased, tilting her face up to his.

'I thought you wanted a marriage of convenience, Christos.'

'Despite appearances, I was never that much of a fool. I want and always have wanted a marriage with you in it,' he said simply. 'It's the only way it works for me.'

She smiled up at him, love shimmering in her eyes. 'Good—because I'm in this for the long haul.'

'And I intend to make it a pleasurable journey for us all,' he promised, laying a protective hand on her stomach.

Her throat thick with emotion, she covered his hand with her own and intertwined her fingers with his. 'Any place you go, I'll quite happily follow.'

EPILOGUE

WHEN Becca returned from her appointment she ran straight out onto the terrace, impatient to share her news with Christos. It was the sort of news that deserved to be shouted from the roof—and here that was an option.

That was why she loved their beach villa here on the island so much. There were no servants to be guarded or circumspect around, no formality, no ringing phones—just them: the family.

And she knew that Christos treasured the time they spent here as much as she did.

She gave a sigh of sheer pleasure as she looked out to the beach and the sea beyond. And—right in the middle— the three people that made it very, *very* good to be Becca Carides! She lifted her hand and waved wildly.

Down on the beach, Christos caught his breath at the sight of the slim figure with her hand above her head. As he lifted his own hand to shade his eyes the soft summer breeze caught the full skirt of the dress she wore. He smiled and felt the familiar lick of lust as he watched her strenuous efforts to subdue the billowing fabric as it lifted.

Becca gave up on controlling her dress and, slipping the straps over her shoulders, let it fall to the ground. Underneath she wore a bright red bikini, which she had brought along for the long weekend because Christos liked the way it clashed with her hair. *She* liked what he said it did to his blood pressure!

She bent over to unfasten the ankle straps on her sandals, and saw the tall, tanned figure loping up the beach to meet her.

There had to be very few men who looked as good as her husband in a pair of swimming shorts, Becca reflected. Long legs, broad shoulders, and a taut, toned body that carried not an ounce of excess flesh to hide the perfect musculature she never tired of looking at.

I just love the way he moves.

Becca smiled as she realised anyone hearing her panting would assume she had been the one doing the running.

'Where have you been?' Christos demanded, placing the giggling bundles he carried, one under each arm, on the tiled terrace floor.

He lifted his head and, grinning at his wife, adopted a long-suffering tone as he added, 'And before you ask—yes I did keep them out of the midday sun, smother them with suncream and keep their hats on at all times… Well, *almost* all times,' he corrected, pulling a frilled sunhat from the auburn curls of their eleven-month-old daughter. With a gummy grin she immediately snatched it from his hand with her chubby baby fingers.

'How like a woman,' he observed, straightening up and pressing a hungry kiss on his wife's lips. 'Mmm—you taste good,' he said, before wagging a finger at their daughter and complaining, 'She spends all morning pulling it off. Now she decides she wants it.' He tapped their daughter's tip-tilted nose playfully and looked around for her brother.

'Vasilis!' he called. 'Where is that boy?'

Laughing as she gathered her grubby, rosy-cheeked daughter into her arms, Becca pointed across the terrace.

She would imagine there were many people who would have difficulty connecting this figure with sand in his hair and a relaxed grin on his face with the man who wore designer suits and never had a hair out of place. That man could sway a boardroom with a well-chosen sentence and one of his signature looks.

'*Theos!*' Christos exclaimed. 'Imagine how fast he's go

ing to move when he finally decides to walk!' Christos moved to retrieve Vasilis before he managed to catch the cat he was pursuing. 'When are you going to catch up with your sister, Vasilis?' Christos demanded of their son, who had yet to take his first step.

'He'll get there,' Becca said comfortably, as she watched Christos heave the struggling little boy into his arms. The similarity between father and son was marked—the only real difference being that Vasilis had deep blue eyes…her eyes. It was his twin sister who had inherited their father's dark brown eyes.

'Girls mature much faster. You remember that, Effy,' she told her daughter, who was attempting to eat her hat. 'You know, I think she's teething again.'

Christos rolled his eyes to the ceiling and groaned. 'Will there ever be a time when one of them isn't?'

Becca laughed. At moments like this it hit her just how lucky she was. A deep sense of contentment washed over her as Christos joined her.

'You look very pleased with yourself,' he observed.

'Actually, I *am* pretty pleased with myself,' she said, offering her lips for the lingering kiss her husband planted on them.

'Yes, *very* good—like strawberries.' He studied her bright eyes and prettily flushed cheeks with narrowed eyes. 'Has this smugness and sparkle got something to do with your mysterious appointment this morning?'

'You could say that,' she confirmed. Then, unable to stretch out the tension another second, she blurted, 'The doctor confirmed what I already knew…I'm pregnant, Christos. We're going to have another baby!'

Christos stilled, his eyes dropping down her slim body. 'We've only just started trying,' he protested hoarsely. 'I thought these things took time.'

'You of all people should know that isn't always so.'

Her shoulder lifted in a shrug. 'I suppose we just have to accept that you're a regular superstud.'

'A baby...' he said, still looking stunned.

Becca nodded, then blinked as without a word he took the placid Effy from her arms and planted both twins in their toy-filled playpen. Striding urgently back to his wife's side, he took her face between his hands.

There was a shade of anxiety in his face as he asked, 'This is what you want, *yineka mou*?'

Becca covered his hands with her own. 'I've never been happier in my life, Christos,' she admitted. 'And you?'

Christos's eyes were suspiciously bright as he brought her hands to his lips and pressed a fervent kiss on first one small palm and then the other. 'If you find a happier man than me he is lying—because it simply is not possible.'

The depth of sincerity shining in his eyes brought an emotional lump to her throat.

'I love you so much it hurts,' she admitted thickly.

His eyes burning, Christos bent his head and kissed her with a passion that made Becca's toes curl.

When he lifted his head she released a shuddering sigh. 'You have no idea how glad I am that you came back for Alex's wedding... When I think about not meeting you...'

His strong hands closed possessively over the rounded contours of her firm bottom and Becca leaned into him, loving the lean, male hardness of his body.

'There was no chance of that not happening.'

'No...?'

He shook his head and said, with total conviction, 'You and I were fated to be together.'

Becca blinked away the emotional tears that sprang to her eyes. 'You really believe that, don't you?' she said, wonder in her eyes as she stroked the strong curve of his lean cheek.

'Don't you?' he challenged.

A smile of sheer happiness illuminated her flushed face as she dragged his head down to hers. 'I think there's a special someone for everyone, but only the lucky few find each other. And I'm the luckiest—to have found you.'

THREE MORE FREE BOOKS!

HARLEQUIN *Presents*

This September, purchase 6 Harlequin Presents books and get these THREE books for FREE!

IN THE BANKER'S BED
by Cathy Williams

CITY CINDERELLA
by Catherine George

AT THE PLAYBOY'S PLEASURE
by Kim Lawrence